A Second Chance in Paradise

By

Tom Winton

ALSO BY TOM WINTON

www.TomWintonAuthor.com

Beyond Nostalgia
The Last American Martyr
Four Days with Hemingway's Ghost
Within a Man's Heart
The Voice of Willie Morgan and Two Other Short Stories

ISBN-13: 978-1494262556

ISBN-10: 149426255X

A Second Chance in Paradise is a fictional work. All the names, characters, events and locations are from the author's imagination or are used fictitiously. Any resemblance to current events or locations or living persons, is entirely coincidental.

Special thanks to Sessha Batto for designing my book cover and to Kristen Stone for all her help with the editing.

Chapter 1

For better or for worse, certain events remain clear in our minds forever. Not only can we pull up visions of those memorable moments at will, but we can also rekindle the emotions we *felt* when we lived them. Granted, whether they were happy emotions or sad ones, ecstatic or devastating, we may not be able to bring them back with all their initial impact, but we can still feel them. Believe me, it's true. I know all too well. I have one particular memory that to this day, twenty-one years later, still rips away another piece of my heart every time it invades my mind.

Clustered beneath a white comforter the way we were that early morning, Wendy and I resembled a single drift of the snow that was soon to fall. Outside our tract house, the darkness and stars were about to surrender to morning's first light. All over Smithtown alarm clocks tore into people's sleep, lights came on, toilets flushed, and coffee brewed. Yes, the winter sky over our Long Island town was cloudless, but that would soon change. Also on the cusp of change, though I hadn't a clue, was the course of my life.

It started out like any other morning when still in a semiconscious state after silencing the alarm clock, I got out of bed first. Arms outstretched in the darkness, palms up, I followed my bare feet across the carpet, feeling for the bathroom door. As I began my morning rituals, all of them involving running water, Wendy pulled my pillow over her head as she always did. It hadn't dawned on me yet but the date was February 22nd – my thirty-ninth birthday.

After I finished doing everything I had to, I quietly padded back into the bedroom. I put on my gray pinstriped suit with the "slightly irregular" stamped over the inside pocket, a white oxford shirt from Penney's, and a burgundy tie. In the dim light beginning to seep through the curtains I watched myself in the mirror as I tied a Windsor knot.

The salesman's dreaded uniform, I thought. *What a waste of time this charade is. No matter how hard we work, Wendy and I still keep getting knocked back farther and farther. I am so sick and tired of worrying about money.*

Easing up to the dresser mirror then, I carefully assessed myself.

At a shade over six feet tall, people often told me I was broad at the shoulders. Despite the extra half inch I couldn't shake from my waist, the three weekly trips I was making to the gym were paying off. I still had a good head of hair too, despite the few pesky strands of gray that had recently homesteaded up there. I was reasonably content with my face and most women didn't seem to find it objectionable either. But that didn't matter. I loved Wendy too much to be interested in anyone else. The bridge of my nose had been a bit out of kilter for years, but you'd almost have to be looking for the flaw to notice it. It had been broken at a dance club when I was nineteen – after being sucker-punched by a guy with bad judgment. By the time that fight was broken up, the instigator looked far worse than I did.

"Are you getting up, Wendy?" I asked, finger-combing my hair one last time.

"No," came her muffled voice from beneath my foam pillow, "I'm going to have to call in sick today, Sonny. I just can't seem to shake this cold. It's been what ... three days now?"

Picking up one end of the pillow, I leaned over and kissed my wife's bed-warmed cheek. Then, while still holding the pillow, I straightened up and marveled for the thousandth time at how enchanting she still was. We had no children. Wendy was unable to. But kids or no kids, most women her age and many much younger would have given their entire wardrobes and more to look as good as she did. As I stood there a few seconds, I experienced one of those fleeting isolated moments in a busy man's life when he truly appreciates what's most important to him.

Seventeen years we're married, I thought, *and she still doesn't look much different than she did back in high school.*

"You stay in bed, hon." I said, smoothing back a fallen wisp of her long, auburn hair from her forehead. "I'll call your office later. I'll tell Silverman you're not going to make it in."

Hearing my last words, Wendy's emerald eyes suddenly flashed wide open. She jerked her head up as if she'd heard a middle-of-the-night burglar tampering with a window.

"No!" she said, with a peculiar amount of urgency before altering her tone and going on, "No ... it's OK Sonny. I'm up now anyway. I'll call him when the office opens."

"Alright, alright," I said, my eyes narrowing a bit. "I'll see you around 6:30. I don't have to work out today so I'll come right home. Call you later."

I then stepped out of the bedroom, slowly easing the door closed behind me.

When I walked into the kitchen, I saw two unopened envelopes on the counter. Inside them were more bills. One was past due with a late charge added to it; the other from a plumber for an unexpected three-hour visit the previous week. He wanted *four-hundred dollars.* As I turned on the coffeemaker, all I could do was shake my head.

After drinking some of the coffee and eating breakfast, I backed my aging blue van out of the driveway and slowly motored down New Bridge Street. Steering between the two close rows of small Cape Cod style homes – each identical except for the color of their paint – it dawned on me that it was my birthday. Immediately I thought it odd that Wendy hadn't wished me a happy one. In the past she'd always gone out of her way to make all my birthdays feel special. And that bothered me during the entire drive to work.

"Come on," I said aloud, as if trying to convince myself, "she had just opened her eyes! And she wasn't feeling good."

I finally blew it off when I turned the van into the North Island Mall's parking lot and motored slowly to the far end of the freestanding city of retail mega-giants. Macy's, Penney's, Bloomingdale's, all of them were part of the behemoth concrete island that to shopaholics rose like Oz from the sprawling field of parking spaces. Early as it was, with nary a car in the lot, the place looked about as lively as a deserted cemetery. For some reason, and it was the first time ever, all the cement car-stops sitting back-to-back put me to mind of headstones – wide, low headstones.

I don't know what came over me, but for no obvious reason I suddenly got this very eerie feeling. I quickly eased the van into a spot, killed the engine, and then it really hit me. No, it *slammed* me. WHAMMO – just like that, I felt as if something horrible was about to happen to me. Other than the cold, gloomy, overcast weather, I couldn't for the life of me fathom what brought it on. Never before had I felt this anxious – this panicky. It was as if my subconscious mind had withdrawn itself from my body, risen to the top of one of the parking lot's tall, lofty light posts, and was staring at me through the windshield – *cackling* down at me.

I've got to get out of this van! Got to get some air! Oh shit ... my hands are trembling. My palms are sweating, too. What in the hell is going on here?

I climbed out of the van so quickly I hit my head on the top of the doorjamb. The instant my feet hit the ground the wind suddenly began to gust harder, bringing with it the predicted storm's first white flakes. Without looking back, I slammed the door and double-timed it toward Searcy's Furniture World. The store was only a hundred yards away, yet to me it appeared to be far off on the horizon. Head down, as I made my way across the lot, I wrestled with my mind, trying to pull myself together. But it continued to play its tricks.

Oh shit ... am I having a heart attack? That's it! It feels like it's going to thump right through my ribs. My temples are pounding, too. Oh God, this is it. Please. Please, no! It can't be. I'm only thirty-eight

... I mean thirty-nine. I've got to get inside that store, fast!

Upping my pace to just short of a run, snow now beginning to accumulate on my eyebrows, I admitted to myself that I had really been stressed out lately, mostly about money. I realized for the first time that that necessary evil, or the lack of it I should say, had been consuming me. But that revelation was short-lived.

Okay, you're almost there now. I thought, *Please God, no! Don't let this be the end. Don't let me die here. What'll Wendy do without ... oh no! No! Now I'm feeling dizzy. I think my vision is blurring, too. I feel like I can only see straight ahead, like I'm looking into a tunnel. I'm going to fall flat on my face, I know it. It's like I have vertigo. Shit, I've got to get to that door, fast.*

I did. I made it. And the moment I reached the store's double glass doors, I muttered, "Oh God ... thank you! Thank you so much!

Like violent storms sometimes do this terrifying experience subsided as suddenly as it had arrived. It may have been short-lived, but it had been far too intense for my liking. I took it as a warning sign. Right then and there I vowed to lighten up on myself. I was going to try not to take things so seriously anymore. To hell with money, debt, and all the rest that goes with it, whatever was going to be was going to be. I decided I wasn't going kill myself with worry. At least I was going to try not to.

Surrounded by almost an acre of furniture inside the store, I hustled up the long center aisle toward the sales counter in back. Though still somewhat spooked, I was so glad to be back in touch with reality that I didn't even notice the acrid smell of the dyes and formaldehyde in all the furniture that always, by day's end, made my eyes look as if they'd spent far too much time in an over-chlorinated swimming pool.

"You'd better hustle your sweet little behind into the conference room, handsome," said Fran, the bleached-blond, gum-snapping cashier who, at thirty-one, had already worn out three husbands. "Halstead's already started his 'motivational' meeting and ... hey, wow, wait a minute! Are you okay, Sonny? You don't look so hotsy totsy today."

Still hustling as I turned left at the counter, glancing at my Casio and feeling Fran's eyes all over my behind, I said, "*I'm fine*, Franny! Just didn't get a good night's sleep is all."

A few steps later I leaned into the ornate mahogany door that lead into the conference room. As it was at all our meetings, all the salespeople were seated alongside the long mica table and Ronald Halstead stood at the head of it, rambling on about something. Stopping his spiel as I entered, he turned toward me, put on a frown, and snarled, "Glad to see you could make it today, *Mister* Raines."

In no mood for his nonsense after what I'd just been through in the parking lot, I stepped lively to a vacant chair at the far end of the table. All the salespeople's eyes followed me. A few whispered comments to the person next to them. Surely they were making cracks about how bad I looked.

Halstead, a onetime Hofstra University linebacker by this time crowding fifty, and three hundred pounds, went right back into his act. All decked-out in a royal blue suit with a white carnation, a pink shirt with huge, faux gold cufflinks, and a bright red "power tie," he stood up there as erect as his sagging body would allow. Gut sucked in, chest all puffed out, he strutted back and forth like ruptured over-the-hill gamecock.

Halstead, who worked sixty-plus hours every week and was paid only for forty, simply couldn't comprehend why none of his fourteen salespeople would do the same. He was one of those born-for-retail types the big chains loved to hire. They gave him a title, let him think he's going places then worked him so hard he didn't know what day of the week it was. The corporate strategy obviously worked in Halstead's case because twice within the previous two months he had come in on a Tuesday – not realizing it was his day off.

Minutes after I sat down the usual glum mood in the conference room nosedived even further. Halsted began reading everybody's sales totals for the previous three months. The numbers were abysmal, but it wasn't the salespeople's fault. Times had gotten bad. Folks simply weren't buying furniture.

Nevertheless, as if Halstead were addressing a room full of mindless idiots, he announced, "And *there* people ... lies the problem. We are not meeting our sales quotas! You *must* bring up your numbers! Would you please tell me *what* seems to be the problem here? Can anybody tell me?"

As I took this all in, hot perspiration surfaced beneath my collar. I could feel myself tightening up again too. Some serious anger was building up quickly. Thinking how difficult things had become for Wendy and me, my pulse quickened as well. I just had to do something. I couldn't sit there and listen to this off-the-wall finger pointing. Everyone in the room, Halstead included, knew why sales were down. We were in the midst of the deepest recession in decades.

Soon I'd had enough of Halstead's nonsensical blabbering. Sick and tired of not only losing the war but every small battle as well, I rolled my eyes at all the people sitting around the table. As always, nobody was going to refute this foolishness. Nobody had the nerve. Nobody but me, that is. In a single motion I shoved the seat out from beneath me and rose to my feet. Still surveying my colleagues, carefully measuring every word, I blurted, "Maybe all the rest of you are afraid to speak up, but I'm sure as hell not. I've had it!"

I took one deep breath, swiveled my head toward the store manager, then went on, "Who are you trying to snow, Halstead? The reason our numbers are down and none of us are making even half a living is because *you* load the sales floor!"

For the second time in twenty minutes my hands began to tremble. But this time it wasn't caused by anxiety or panic. This was different. Adrenaline provoked this shake, just like it sometimes had when I was growing up, back in Queens. Times when angry words precluded some pretty rough and tumble street fights. But this time, here in the conference room, I kept my clenched fists at my sides, trying hard to squeeze the shake out of them as I went on.

"Three months ago you hired five additional bodies – which was the last thing we needed in this soft market. Hell, it was tough enough when there were only nine of us on the showroom floor. *Then* ... what did you do after that? You cut our commissions from five to four percent!"

I dropped my head, rotated it twice then looked

back over at Halstead, scorching him with my eyes. Next I pointed at him, started shaking my index finger as if I'd just burnt it and went on, "Let me tell you something, my heartless friend ... *you're* the reason we're making crap ... you and Searcy's!"

"Raines," Halstead snapped, "I want you in my office right after this meeting. And if you hope to stay here for the remainder of it, just sit there and be quiet! Do not interrupt me again! We don't need any more of your negative outbursts."

With that, the room filled with excited whispers. Most of the salespeople seemed to be loving all this early morning action.

"No! I don't think so, Halstead!" I shot back now. "I'm not shutting up this time. And you know what, FREAK your office. Why don't you just come over here and kiss my ass instead? After all, that's the kind of thing you're good at. And let me tell you something else before you get some sick satisfaction out of firing me ... I QUIT! I'M OUT OUTTA HERE! Working in this place is like ... like mental masturbation. It's a freaking joke, a bad joke."

With all that finally off my chest after keeping it inside for so long, I barged right the hell out of that kangaroo court. Fighting with myself as I stormed across the showroom toward the front exit, I somehow managed not to turn around. I really wanted to bust right back into that conference room and give Halstead more than words to remember me by. But I didn't.

Pushing through both glass doors at once, I bowed my head right into an onslaught of wind-driven snow. It was heavy now. The flakes were the size of nickels and plenty damp. Two inches of the thick white stuff had already accumulated on the ground, and the best I could do was to slowly shuffle my way across the slippery lot. When I finally made it to my van, I cranked her up and turned on the heater. Immediately it blew warm air. I hadn't been inside Searcy's Furniture World for very long.

I forged toward home as quickly as I safely could. Steering stiffly, driving ever so carefully through the deepening snow, my only thoughts were of Wendy. Over and over I rehearsed how I was going to break the news to her. Once I said aloud, "Should I tell her I got fired or tell her the truth?" But I knew damn well what I'd do. I couldn't lie to her. I never had before. I'd have to fess up. I may have had my fair share of shortcomings but dishonesty wasn't one of them.

A half hour after leaving the store I turned right onto New Bridge Street. Like all the rest of Long Island, my neighborhood was now blanched white with clean, fresh snow. Slowly, I motored up the residential street until I was about a half block away from my house. Then I noticed something odd. A gold car, it looked like a Lexus, was pulling away from the curb near my house. It seemed to be right in front of it. Next to nobody on the block ever parked in the street. All the houses had their own driveways. Moments later, I slowed to a stop before pulling into my driveway. Sure enough, alongside the curb was a perfectly dry, dark asphalt rectangle where the Lexus had been parked.

Who the hell could that have been? I wondered, the fresh snow mashing beneath my wheels as I rolled into the driveway.

I killed the ignition, climbed out and closed the door ever so gently. Then I trudged through the five inches of white stuff to where the car had been parked. With a cold mist now escaping my nostrils with every quickening breath, I noticed there were footprints on the front yard. About the same size as my own, just one set, they were fresh as can be – and those tracks led from the front door to exactly where I was standing at the curb. Whoever had been inside the house had been there a while.

With my mind whizzing around in all different directions, I made my way across the small front yard to the door, carefully avoiding the footprints as if they were HIV-positive. I climbed the three steps, entered the house and closed the door firmly – making sure the act was audible. Then I just stood there. I didn't move a muscle or make another sound. All I could hear was the ticking clock in the living room and the sound of my molars grinding. In the excruciating silence my heart thumped hard against my ribs, and I felt hot blood pulsating in my temples.

God, I hope she has a legitimate excuse! She must have! But how can that be possible? Hayley and Marlene are the only of Wendy's friends who ever stop over here. Neither of them could ever afford to drive a Lexus, and their feet, they must be six sizes smaller than those prints outside. Ohhh shit, no! She's my wife, my mate, my confidante and partner. We've been together all our adult lives. She's been part of me the whole time – the best part of me. Why would she ever ...

Abruptly, my thoughts ended there. The sound of creaking springs cut them short. It was Wendy, climbing out of our bed.

Padding up the short hallway toward the living room, still out of sight, she said, "Steve? Is that you? Did you forget something?"

It had been her boss, Steve Silverman.

My heart stuttered as I stood there, breathless now. My wind-chilled face contorted as if I were experiencing some horribly painful physical torture. I'd have preferred that any day. That I could take – anything but this!

I stood there motionless, my back against the door, listening to Wendy's steps as she made her way down the short hallway.

Then she stepped into the living room – completely naked.

Seeing now that it was me, not Steve Silverman, the smile on her face instantly drooped. Her lips parted slightly, as if she were going to say something, explain, but she didn't. She just froze.

This was it – I was living out the worst nightmare any caring husband could imagine. Some men may think of this dreaded scenario often, others rarely, but, no matter what the frequency, if and when it happens, if a man truly loves his women, it is the most devastating of all human experiences. It can cripple the ego, no, worse than that, far worse, when the husband worships his wife the way I had.

Through glazed eyes I stood surveying my wife, who stood there, totally undressed for another man. My eyes moved to all the places that, before today, only I had ever touched, fondled, kissed and entered. The creamy flesh of her soft, erect breasts; her impossibly trim waist; the tantalizing curve of her hips; the triangular patch of silky, auburn hair where the inside of her thighs met.

"My good God, Wendy! What have you done? Why would you ever do something like this? How in the hell could you?"

She said nothing. Arms still at her sides, she turned her palms out and opened her mouth to speak. But nothing came out.

A long moment passed, an agonizing moment neither of us would ever forget. Then, startled by my own calmness, disappointed by it, I began to weigh my few options as I continued to stare at her in disbelief.

Do I kill her, right here and now? Do I go get that bastard Silverman? Should I kill them both?

Slowly but deliberately – as if in a trance, I approached her. With each small step my tormented eyes cut deeper into hers. They spoke to her – cried out to her, and she understood them. They told her what she had done to me. They told her my heart felt like it was being wrenched by a thousand savage hands.

Face to face now, close enough to smell the familiar scent of her bare skin, the shock, hurt, and profound sense of loss I'd felt suddenly vanished. Contempt kicked in. I was now working – working *hard* to fight back my rage.

Through quivering lips, with my voice breaking, I managed to say, "I hope you enjoyed yourself, Wendy. You've given me onc hell of a birthday gift."

After that I dropped my eyes from hers and gave my wife one long, last look – head to toe and back again. In a tone drenched with hurt, sorrow, regret and a host of other miserable emotions I said, "Have a nice life ... Wendy." Then, as I brushed past her, I shouted so loud that the fogged-up windows vibrated, "NOW, GET THE FUCK OUT OF MY WAY!"

I stormed down the hallway, into the bedroom, and started packing everything except my business suits. Those I would leave behind.

"That's it, I'm finished with these!" I muttered to myself, realizing I needed to do something else with my life. But still, as I struggled to lock the two overstuffed suitcases lying on that tainted bed, I felt like I might vomit. Strengthened by my rage, I managed to close the luggage and snap them shut. There would be no coming back and I knew it.

On my way out the front door, I stopped to look at her one last time. Still stark naked, she looked so pitiful. Slumped down on our plaid sofa; streams of tears and mascara networking down her cheeks, she sobbed, "Sonny ... I am so sorry." She then hung her head and shook it as she reflected, "It's just ... just that with you working evenings and weekends all these years and with all the money problems we've had, we ... we've drifted apart, somehow."

It was true.

Outside, with the snow still falling, I loaded my belongings into the van. I opened the garage door, grabbed all my fishing rods, threw them in the back of the van, cleared off the windows, cranked up the engine and, for the last time, drove away from 902 New Bridge Street. Looking into the fogged-up rear-view mirror, I watched my home and my past life shrink out of sight.

Then I lost it. I wept profusely, tasting the saltiness of my tears as I drove on.

Chapter 2

I didn't confront Steve Silverman. I knew if I did, I wouldn't have been able to contain myself. I'd have gone absolutely crazy. Probably would have killed him, gotten locked up, who knows what after that. In modern society, repressed emotions and actions may be considered signs of mature male behavior, but that didn't mean a thing to me. My instincts sent me different signals. I didn't like holding back. Deep inside, it didn't feel natural. The only thing that kept me from paying Silverman a visit was the consequences I would have paid.

I didn't talk to or lay eyes on Wendy for three solid months. Oh, there were times, plenty of them, when I thought, *Damn it all! I don't want to go on another minute like this. I can't. Without her there's nothing in front of me. Ten minutes from now, tomorrow, a year from now – none of it means a damned thing without her. If she's truly sorry; if she wants to get back together, who knows, maybe I could eventually get over what she did to me. Maybe things could someday be the same again.*

But, bad as I wanted to, I never did jump into my van, speed out to Smithtown, bust into 902 New Bridge, and take the love of my life into my arms. Bad as I wanted to, I knew I couldn't. Because every time

I reached the end of that reoccurring thought – the part about eventually getting over Wendy's infidelity – I'd listen to my heart. What was left of it told me, *Forget it Sonny, things can never be the same. You and I will never get over this thing, but we will learn to live with it.*

During the course of those first few months, I'd taken a temporary job painting apartments back in Queens. Bobby Slap, a divorced buddy I grew up with and my closest friend not only put me to work but opened his apartment to me as well. Then, on the last afternoon of my stay, after we'd knocked off of work early, I thanked my good friend one last time.

It was just a few days before Memorial Day weekend, a Tuesday, a glorious Tuesday with a perfect sky and mild spring weather. I was sitting opposite Bobby in his bare-bones living room, sipping Miller-Lite with my lifelong friend. On the opposite wall, above the television's black screen, two pennants hung. White letters on the navy-blue one read "Yankees," and the royal-blue and orange one shouted "New York Mets." Between the two was a framed photograph of the 1971 Bayside High School "Commodores" football team. Front and center, standing on the field side by side, each of us holding a football were Bobby and I. He played quarterback, I was a wide receiver, and we were the team's co-captains.

Through an open window leading to the fire escape, a pleasant spring breeze ruffled the sheer curtains. Coming in with the fresh air were the excited shouts of children playing on the wide sidewalk three stories below. Being city boys, neither Bobby nor I noticed the occasional honking horn or the nonstop, gurgling co-roo-coo of pigeons perched on the iron fire escape.

Keeping my elbow on the arm of the chair I was in, I tilted my beer can in my friend's direction and said, "You know, Bobby ... I owe you one for all you've done for me."

"Don't be a jerk, man. What'd I do for you?"

"Come on. You know what I'm talking about. How could I ever have saved enough to go south without your help? You put me up, for free. You put me to work. I won't forget that."

Bobby took a long gulp of a fresh cold beer then brought his eyes back to mine saying, "Getouttahere, I needed a helper. You needed work. It was a win-win. Besides ... it gets kind of lonely living alone. I hate to say this, but you'll find that out soon enough."

I reached for my cigarettes lying on the garage-sale table alongside the chair, took one out, and without lighting it said, "You know, Bobby, if I made it through these past three months, I think I can make it through anything. You've been there. You know it isn't easy. And don't think I haven't noticed how you've tried to make it easier for me to handle all this time."

"You're nuts," Bobby said, waving me off, turning towards the open window for a second. "I treated you the same as I always have. All we did was work, hang out here, and go out for a few beers now and then. I wasn't babying you."

"Yeah, sure, tough guy. Like you never tried to clear off the road for me, did you?"

"Look, I did whatever I did. That's all there is to it. How's your beer? You need another one? And by the way, you never should have gone back to smoking."

"Yeah, yeah, I know. What can I tell you? I'll get myself a beer in a minute." I said, before lighting up the cigarette, taking a drag and blowing the filtered smoke towards the sixty-year-old ceiling. "You know I'm leaving right after court tomorrow."

"Yeah, I know. Tomorrow's D-day. I'm gonna kinda miss you being around here, always being in the way, you pain in the ass."

With a broad smile rising beneath my new moustache, I said, "Yeah, I know. But this is what I want to do right now. This is what I *need* to do right now. You remember when we were kids – those times my parents took me to Fort Lauderdale. I had the time of my life down there. The eternal sunshine, all that blue water full of fish, palm trees, suntan oil, it was great. Then when ... when Wendy and I went to Key West on our honeymoon, well, that was it. I was hooked."

"Hell yes, I remember you going down to Lauderdale." Bobby said, purposely not mentioning the part about Wendy and me. "I hated you for it. I was one jealous SOB."

"Do you remember the time my parents offered to take you with us?"

"Sure do. I'll never forget that one. We were about fourteen. It took me weeks to talk my mother into letting me go. Then what happens! Two days before we're supposed to leave she changes her mind. She said she'd worry herself sick. Guess it was a good thing I didn't go. It was only about a month later that she had her first nervous breakdown."

"Yeah," I said, "thank God she's doing better nowadays.

My best friend, this man I shared a thousand memories with, looked at me pensively. My look at him lingered as well. Nodding my head ever so slowly I knew exactly what he was thinking when I said, "Look, man, I've got to give this Florida thing a shot. If it doesn't work out, I'll be back."

"If you do, you know you can stay here as long as you have to."

"Thanks, man. You're the greatest."

"Oh stop! Don't be getting all sappy on me now because you're gonna be leaving"

Shortly before ten the next morning my divorce was finalized at a courthouse in Hauppauge, Long Island. And not once during the proceedings did I allow myself to make eye contact with Wendy. I just couldn't. Angry as I was at her, I knew if our eyes met it would only have intensified the hurt I was just learning to live with. Sitting in that cold, legal, strictly-business courtroom wasn't easy. I wanted to scream at Wendy, so loud that the walls would shake. I wanted to jump up from my wooden chair and give her all kinds of hell. I wanted to dash past the judge's bench, shove my wife's damned lawyer on his ass, throw my arms around her and whisk her the hell out of there. I wanted to take her home and go on with our lives just the way we did before the morning of my birthday. But none of that happened. I stayed in my seat and did what I had to. When it was finally over, I simply stood up, about-faced, and strode to the exit door.

It took me five minutes to walk to the parking lot where my van was waiting – gassed up, tuned up, and loaded up. I turned the key, took one long deep breath then began my 1500 mile journey south, to Key West, Florida.

Chapter 3

Down in the lower reaches of the Florida Keys, a bit south of Big Pine, there's a speck of an island called Wreckers Key. Roughly 100 miles below the mainland – linked to it by a long chain of bridges, it lies inconspicuously between the Atlantic Ocean and The Gulf of Mexico. A one-square-mile island full of lush tropical flora and just a handful of residents, it was originally settled on by a ship-salvaging hermit named Thaddeus Bell.

Legend has it that on stormy nights, during lean times when wrecks were scarce, Bell would ride his horse along the white, sandy shoreline while displaying a bright kerosene lantern. To the wooden ships offshore this moving light appeared to be another ship, and seeing its glow in the darkness, the light gave many a hapless captain a false sense of security. Since there were no lighthouses marking the shallow, treacherous reefs back in the 1830's, this trick worked far more often than one would think. Time and time again an imprudent skipper, thinking he was still in deep water, would steer his vessel too close to shore, only to run helplessly aground on the shallow coral reef that stretches the full length of these Florida Keys.

At first light on the morning after each wreck, old

Thaddeus would take his salvage boat out into the Atlantic and proceed to claim its cargo. And only after the survivors loaded everything of value onto his boat would he take them to safety in Key West. It was all perfectly legal, except of course the part with the horse and lantern.

Almost two centuries later the few inhabitants of Wreckers Key still enjoyed the rare sense of freedom that lawlessness and detachment from modern society affords. This state of mind, along with the key's unfettered beauty is what attracted each and every independent soul who called this subtropical utopia home. Other than Pa Bell and his son Buster, all the other residents of the tiny island had drifted down from states "up north." They'd done this for personal reasons and, collectively, to escape what they saw as the meaningless, robotic existences they had been living in other places.

Fall-down tired after two-and-a-half days on the road, I steered my minivan into the marl parking lot of a shabby convenience store on Wrecker's Key. With crushed shells crunching beneath my wheels, I slowly pulled up to a 1950's era Texaco gas pump – the one without a scrawled, cardboard "out of order" sign on it. Squeezing the nozzle's handle, starting to pump unleaded, I leaned back against the van and studied the gray, weathered, clapboard building before me. *Looks like one of those old feed stores they have up in New England*, I thought. Side by side, two businesses sat beneath the same roof. The faded plywood sign over one read, "Wreckers Key Grocery" the other, "Barnacle Bell's Bar." Dragging the palm of my hand across my already damp forehead, I squinted through the blinding sunlight, watching heat vapors dance upward from the old shingles on the roof. Shifting my eyes a bit, I saw some huge gumbo limbo trees to the side and behind the low-slung building, dwarfing it, giving it an oasis-like appearance. The peculiar trees held my attention with their red flaking trunks. I'd never seen them before and had no idea the locals called them "Tourist Trees" because of the bark's resemblance to peeling sunburnt skin.

After filling the tank, I hung the nozzle back up and went inside to pay. With the wooden screen door creaking closed behind me, I saw a young girl with long, sun-bleached hair standing behind a worn counter. Wearing faded denim cutoffs and a pink halter, with her back to me, she was slowly refilling a cigarette rack. I stood there a moment, seemingly unnoticed, surveying the low-beamed ceiling and sparse shelves. She still didn't turn around or acknowledge me so I just let my stiff, tired legs carry me to the back of the store. From the cold water of a "Coca Cola" cooler far older than I was, I fished a bottle of Gatorade out from beneath two miniature icebergs then creaked across the wooden floor, back to the counter where the girl was still stuffing cigarettes. Her back was still to me.

"Excuse me," I said, "can I have a pack of Carlton 100's in a box ... please?"

Though she turned around slowly, indignantly, she seemed to blush slightly when she looked at me. Then, with a bit of interest, she said, "Oh sure, how much gas did you pump?"

I said "Thirty-four fifty," but was thinking, *That's weird. She took my word for it. That would never happen back in New York.*

Punching keys on an ancient NCR, she casually said, "Hope you're not heading for Key West."

"As a matter of fact I am. Why? What's up?" In my dog-tired condition, I had no room for bad news.

"You got reservations?"

"No. Why?"

"Heard before on the radio that every motel from Key West clear up to Key Largo is full up." Then, in a motherly fashion far too mature for her years, the girl said, "*You know* this is Memorial Day weekend, don't you?"

"Yes I do. *So*?" I came back, shrugging my shoulders.

"On any of the big holidays, you can't get a room nowhere 'round here without advance notice."

"Are you serious?"

"As a heart attack."

"No rooms anywhere?"

"A lot of places are booked a whole year in advance."

"Fantastic. That's just wonderful," I said, my tone weary, defeated. "I've been on the road three days now. I'm burnt out. Now I'll have to sleep in my freaking van? Shit, what's next?"

"That'll be $41.92 please," she said.

With a road-grimy hand, I extracted a wad of bills from the front pocket of my jeans. I peeled off three new twenties from the final withdrawal I'd made from Long Island Savings and Loan – twenty-two hundred dollars – that's all there had been.

The girl flashed a look at me, counted the change into my hand, and looked up at me again. I managed a hint of a smile then headed for the door.

"Wait a sec," her voice suddenly came from behind me. "I can ask Pa Bell if he'd be willing to rent you Mr. Doyle's trailer. He don't usually rent short term, but who knows."

"Who's Pa Bell? And where's this trailer?"

"Oh, Pa's a great old guy. He owns this here store, the bar next door, and the trailer park – the only things on the whole key. Yeah, there's a little bitty park behind this here building, back in the woods a ways. The sign out front of the parking lot says so, but you can't see it. Pa ain't trimmed the hibiscuses in so long they've damn near covered the whole thing up. I love them pretty red flowers, and there's a mama Mockingbird nesting in there too. She's got two young'uns so there's no way Pa'd trim it down now. Besides, even when you *could* see that old sign, most folks didn't stop here anyway, not with Key West only 20 minutes down the road."

"Well ... if you don't mind, maybe you could ask him, but I wouldn't want to impose."

"Never hurts to ask, I always say. C'mon, he's next door."

As we walked to "Barnacle Bell's Bar," I noticed that the girl was barefoot and had a small, red rose tattooed above her left ankle. Glancing at her angelic face alongside me, her features put me to mind of a teenage Sally Fields; cute smile, dimples and all. She was cute as a button. Even the slightly-chipped tooth I'd noticed inside the store didn't take all that much away from her.

Coming in from the hot Florida sun, the dark, cave-like barroom was refreshingly cool. A window-mounted air conditioner whirred as two ceiling fans overhead circulated slowly – Casa Blanca style. There was nobody sitting on any of the dozen or so stools or at the three tables. It had the feel of a place that was just about to open. A few life rings, each with different faded names of boats or ships, hung on the dark wooden walls along with a scattering of fishing rods. Like the vacationers who sometimes stopped into "Barnacle Bell's" I had no way of knowing the planked walls once formed the deck of a Peruvian schooner. There were photographs scattered on the walls here and there, mostly black and whites from the 50's and 60's of successful anglers with phenomenal catches. Baseball great Ted Williams was in one of them. He was holding a thirteen- pound bonefish and standing alongside him was his guide. Though I had no way of knowing it at the time, the man to Williams's left was a very young, and obviously very able, Pa Bell.

Behind the circular bar a tall, solidly-built old man was mopping the Cuban tile floor with what smelled like pine disinfectant. His white brows arched high above two eyes the color of sea water. The deep creases in his forehead attested to his living eighty-two years beneath Florida's unforgiving sun. Studying me as he spoke, he said, "What's up Sissy?" Pa Bell was not one to waste words. He only spoke when he had something to say and then he never rushed into it. He had that slow, easy way of a blue-blooded Conch.

"Pa, this here's, um ... um ... " Sissy stuttered, looking up at me.

"Sonny, Sonny Raines. Glad to meet you," I said, extending my hand over the mahogany bar.

The old sea captain looked directly into my eyes as he slowly took my offering into his own calloused hand. Feeling slightly intimidated as his sausage-like fingers encompassed my hand, I couldn't help but notice the tattooed anchor and "USN" beneath the white hair on his forearm. Like the sign on the front of his building, the image and letters had lost much of their clarity.

"He needs a place to stay, Pa. Everything is filled up already." Sissy said.

"Hmmm ... how long for?"

"Probably just till Monday or Tuesday," I said, "by then I think I'll be able to get something in Key West. That's where I'm headed."

Pa took a long swallow from a can of Busch that was sitting on the bar and after that a hit from a Lucky Strike that had been smoldering in a glass ashtray. With all that out of the way, he said, "I'll rent ya Doyle's Airstream, twenty-five a night. Sissy, take him back to see it. I'll keep an eye on the store."

Desperate for a place to stay, without even seeing

it, I reached in my pocket and said, “I’ll pay you now, I’m sure it’ll be fine.”

“No son,” Pa said, “you ain’t stayed yet, so you don’t owe me nothin’.” Then he began filling a stainless bar cooler with cans of Bud. With his head bowed now, the back of his wide neck put me to mind of the dried and cracked red Georgia clay I’d seen alongside the highway the day before.

Once we were outside again, Sissy climbed into the van with me to show the way to the trailer. With a trail of hot, white dust rising behind us, we drove past the hibiscus-shrouded sign and turned down an unpaved road alongside the store. A few hundred yards back through slash pines and saw palmettos she directed me to turn right. A moment later the trees opened into a clearing and an aging, yet homey little trailer park appeared. About a dozen single-wide mobile homes and travel trailers sat side by side each other in a half-moon configuration. Although the aluminum dwellings were decades old, they were all neat and tidy, and each of them allowed their occupants an unobstructed, million-dollar view. Just steps from their doors there was a narrow strip of beach bordering acres and acres of shallow, gin-clear tropical water. Farther out, beyond the tidal flats, the deep aquamarine waters of Wreckers Channel flowed gently with the slackening tide.

Taking this all in from beneath a canopy of tall

coconut palms, I couldn't help feeling like a modern-day Robinson Crusoe.

"Wow," I said to Sissy, "look at all these coconuts lying around here. Are they diseased or something?"

"Diseased?" Sissy said, scrunching up her face, yanking her chin in, "What the heck are you talking about – diseased?"

"Oh! Sorry, nothing! I didn't mean the place is diseased or anything like that. It's absolutely gorgeous here. This is unbelievable. It's just that back in New York anything of any value that isn't tied down disappears in no time. If this was back there, those coconuts would have been scoffed up as soon as they hit the sand."

A moment later Sissy directed me to pull alongside one of the trailers, and I obeyed. Looking through the van's windows while rolling to a stop, I couldn't get over how much the travel trailer's bare metal exterior, with its rounded corners, resembled the fuselage of a small airplane.

When we entered the narrow, unlocked doorway the heat only intensified and the odor of dampness and mildew invaded my nostrils. But the place was clean. And there was a window- mounted air-conditioner that I turned on immediately. The compressor may have kicked over grudgingly, but once it did she was humming like a soothing song and spewing cool refreshing air.

Trying not to appear overzealous about the bargain-basement price, I quickly told Sissy that everything looked fine and that I wanted to rent it.

That seemed to make her happy and as she left with a smile, the teenager said, “My real name is Vanessa, but everyone here on the Key calls me Sissy.”

“Is it okay if I call you Sissy, too?” I asked, trying to come across as seriously as I could.

I could tell she liked hearing me say her name, even if I hadn’t called her Vanessa.

“Sure. That’ll be just fine!”

After I thanked her and said goodbye, I watched through a window as she trotted and skipped back toward the store, seemingly unaffected by the heat.

Instinctively, I locked the door before dragging myself directly to the shower. The pressure was low, the water hard and warm, but to me it felt heavenly. After luxuriating for quite some time, I dried off, took two steps down the trailer’s tiny hallway, one more into the bedroom and plopped right onto the mattress. Lying there on my back, clean and content, I drank the no-longer-cold Gatorade and smoked a cigarette. I was tired, but I had finally managed to leave New

York, and the long drive was all but over. I just laid there for a while, enjoying exciting thoughts about finally being in Florida and what the future might hold.

But then things changed. That bright feeling of contentment was suddenly overshadowed by something else. Looking up at the unfamiliar low ceiling above, I now felt misplaced. Painful memories of *that* morning – my last birthday, started rolling through my psyche, shrouding my newfound sense of hope and optimism.

Rolling to my side, watching the green frond of a saw palmetto scratching away at a window the size of a porthole, I thought, *God ... why can't I get over this? Will I ever get over it? I go a few days thinking it's getting easier then, poof, I'm hurting all over again – just as bad as I was in the very beginning. I wonder what Wendy's doing right doing now. How she feels at night when she goes to bed alone. Oh, no ... she's probably still seeing that bastard Silverman. She's probably going to bed with ... oh man, put that out of your mind right now. You don't want to even think about ....*

I went on and on like that until the huge Florida sun melted like hot red lava into the Gulf of Mexico. After that, exhaustion mercifully set in and I fell into a long, deep sleep.

Chapter 4

On my first morning in the Keys, I awoke at dawn's first light. Certainly the incessant hum of the air-conditioner had something to do with it as did a rogue cricket that was holed up somewhere inside the trailer. Feeling much better than I did when closing my eyes the night before, I slid into yesterday's jeans and barefooted it outside.

Listening to the unfamiliar quiet, I stood on the small dewy lawn surveying things again. Maybe thirty yards from where I stood, the flat surface of Wreckers Channel mirrored the early morning's pink blushing sky. Way out near the middle, a large tarpon rolled, exposing its thick, silvery body and slapping the water's surface with its broad tail before disappearing back into the depths. I was ecstatic spotting the awesome fish. I couldn't wait to do battle with one of those so-called "silver kings." I'd read in outdoor magazines how once hooked, they sometimes spend more time jumping out of the water then they do in it. Another tarpon surfaced then, a smaller one, making its own light as the new sun reflected off its armor of silver dollar scales. To the right, out past the US 1 bridge on the eastern side of the island, a white sport fishing boat – a cabin job, slowly made its way out into the Atlantic. There was no way I could have known the boat was named "The Island Belle" and that Buster; Pa Bell's son, was at the helm.

With a fair amount of renewed excitement, I stepped over to the van and started unloading it. First I pulled out the two, green suitcases I'd had since my stint with the Air Force twenty years earlier. I hadn't used them much since my discharge because real vacations had always been an unattainable luxury to me and Wendy. For most of those years, the luggage sat in a corner of our garage.

Next I unloaded my arsenal of fishing outfits, carefully watching the rod tips as I carried them into the trailer. I had everything from ultra-lights to monster-taming winches which, when filled properly, held close to half a mile of heavy line. I was obsessed with fishing and always loved how its calming effect could transform in a flash to heart-pounding, adrenaline pumping excitement. Fishing was as unpredictable as my mood swings. It could both thrill you and disappoint you when a trophy fish hurls its body out of the water, displaying all its magnificence; only to snap the line with one mighty shake of its head. Yes, fishing was one of the two joys I'd never tired of. Unfortunately, the other joy had tired of me.

Hands in my pockets, I took a few steps toward the shoreline. It felt good to walk again, to stretch my legs after being crammed in the van for so long. Like the trailer I was staying in, the one next door was shaded by dense palms. It sat at the very end of the semicircular formation and was the closest to the water's edge. There was a light on inside, and the delicious aroma of freshly-brewed coffee wafted from its open windows. The single-wide mobile home had a screened porch on the side, and there was a faded-blue VW Bug, probably older than my van, parked next to it. I had just glanced at the sandy tracks its tires had worn in the sparse grass when I heard the porch door swing open. Quickly rolling my eyes to the right I saw a woman step outside. She was absolutely stunning.

High-waisted and slender she had on a lightweight denim shirt knotted beneath her breasts, white denim shorts, and no shoes. Smiling now she said in a low voice, as if whispering a secret and being careful not to wake anyone, "Hey, I'll bet you could use some coffee."

I stopped in my tracks, took a quick glance around and said, "Well, I ah ... sure! Why not? I'd really like that, if it isn't any trouble."

Approaching her now I said, "By the way, what exactly does someone who could use some coffee look like? I mean, are there telltale signs?" My response seemed kind of weak as it left my tongue, but it was the best I could muster under the circumstances. This beautiful woman had taken me completely off guard.

She let out a low giggle; then said, "There are no telltale signs, but this island isn't the Big Apple and news travels fast. Sissy told me last night that you arrived in the afternoon and rented Mr. Doyle's trailer next door. Come on in."

And I did. We went into the porch and the totally-unpretentious woman extended her right hand saying, "Julie, Julie Albright, how do you do?" She smiled again, and close as I was I saw two rows of the straightest, whitest teeth I'd ever seen. I picked up her offering and gently shook it a time or two. Not normally "a hand man," I still couldn't help but notice the one I was holding was elegant. Her fingers were long, feminine fingers with perfectly manicured nails. But that didn't surprise me. Even dressed down the way she was, everything about her was graceful.

I managed to say, "I'm Sonny Raines, nice to meet you." But it wasn't easy. Her deep brown, sensuous eyes, ever so sleek at the corners, simply took me hostage. And even though I'd never met this woman she somehow seemed familiar. It was uncanny.

"Well, Sonny Raines," she said now, glancing up at the clear morning sky, "is it going to be *sunny* today or will it *rain*?"

"Verrry funny! You picked right up on that. Obviously you've had some coffee already. It's Sonny with and o and there's an e near the end of Raines. Believe me, when I was a kid I took more than my share of ribbing about that."

"I'm just kidding, Sonny. Have a seat and I'll

bring out the coffee. How do you take it?"

"Just a little cream is fine."

"You bet! Have a seat. I'll be right out."

I lowered myself into one of the two rattan swivel rockers on the porch and looked out toward the placid waters of Wreckers Channel again. Two huge birds, almost as tall as full grown men, fascinated me as they strutted side by side along the beach. But that only lasted a moment or two. Soon the sound of a spoon clinking in cups brought my attention back to the woman inside the trailer – this Julie Albright. I couldn't get over how striking she was, even without makeup on. When we had talked a minute earlier, I'd actually seen my own reflection in her long, lustrous black hair, and the way it hung from a perfect part atop her head, sixties style, it only accentuating the gorgeous features in her delicate face. As for her skin, wow, slightly tanned and flawless it was drawn tightly over well-toned limbs.

When she came out with two cups of steaming hot coffee and put them on the lobster trap/table between the chairs, I noticed a green aluminum ashtray sitting there. I asked her, "Do you mind if I smoke?" She only waved me off and smiled. I took a cigarette out, lit it, and she sat down.

Looking out at my van parked just beyond her VW, she then said, "Looking at all those Love Bugs smeared all over your grill it's obvious you just got down here."

"Yup, like Sissy told you, I just arrived yesterday. I was headed for Key West, but they said on the radio there were no rooms available – with the holiday weekend and all."

I took a sip of the strong coffee, and she said, "More and more people are coming down every year. How long are *you* planning to stay?"

"I'm not sure yet, maybe permanently, maybe not. It depends on how things go. I've got to see if I can find work and get situated."

I then saw Julie take a quick glance my left hand. After that she raised her eyes to my face, appraising it for the second time. Feeling self-conscious, I caught myself fidgeting in my chair like a nervous schoolboy. I straightened up in my chair a bit then took another sip of coffee.

I hated myself for acting that way and was sure she'd picked up on it. I also knew she was trying to make me feel more relaxed when, as if genuinely interested, she asked, "What part of New York are you from?"

"I grew up in Queens, but I've been out on Long Island for fifteen or sixteen years. You're not from New York? I can't detect an accent."

She pivoted her head gently, said, "No," then looked dreamily into the cup she'd been holding. It was strange. She didn't say anything else for a moment. She looked at that coffee as if she could see her past in the hot, brown liquid.

"I grew up in Ft. Lauderdale," she finally said, "but I did live in Manhattan for four years ... on East 89th. That was a while back. Great place, no matter what people from other parts of the country might say. I had a real fun time there." She paused again, looking out at the channel for a few seconds before continuing, "But something came up, and I decided it was time to leave New York."

Her mysterious dark eyes now seemed as though they were watching events from her past life take place all over again. I knew by the way she was winding a strand of long black hair around her slender finger that those events had not been pleasant. But she brought herself back to the here and now. And she asked me, "What brings you to paradise, Sonny Raines?"

I took a sip from my cup and then shrugged, "Just ... just tired of the stress, the winters, the rush-rush pace, and the exorbitant living costs. I'm hoping to simplify things – scale down, live as cheaply as possible. I'm not much for conventionalism. I detested the regimented lifestyle I'd been living."

Julie Albright probably knew by the way I looked out at the water as I spoke that there was more to it than I was letting on to. That there was probably a woman involved. She probably figured that I was yet another casualty of the matrimonial wars. But she didn't try to delve. She let me off the hook by asking, "More coffee?"

"No thanks. I'm good. If you don't mind me asking, how long have you been down here ... in the Keys?"

"Nine years now – right here in this trailer. When I left New York I went back to Lauderdale for six or seven years. It had changed so much since I grew up there. Throngs of people; crime running rampant, you know what they say ... you can never go back. I wanted to find someplace quiet. Soooo," she said while looking beyond the turquoise channel to the uninhabited green shoreline of Flagler Key, "I came down to the Keys and found Wreckers. It was and still is perfect for me."

"Why not Key West? Why a secluded place like this? Don't get me wrong, it's beautiful, but it is really quiet."

"Let's just say I became disillusioned with people. I wanted to be pretty much left alone. If I want to be around crowds, I can always drive south a few minutes. There are always hordes of people on Duval

Street. Anyway, I work in right there in Key West, part time, two days a week. That's enough for me."

"I can appreciate that," I said, now watching a Great Blue Heron snare a finger mullet out on the flats. The long-legged bird flipped the wriggling fish a few times until he finally caught it headfirst in his dagger-like bill, enabling him to ingest it.

At that point, not wanting to wear out my welcome, I stood up and thanked Julie for the coffee. I also told her that since I'd be on the key at least until Monday I was sure I'd be seeing her again.

Looking a bit let down as she rose to her feet, she said, "I hope so." But then her tone perked up and I thought she sounded a bit hopeful when she added, "Say ... why don't you stop by Barnacle Bell's tonight? There's going to be live music and there should be a good *crowd*." She accentuated the word "crowd" with a wide smile then continued, "You could meet some of the folks that live here."

"Barnacle Bell's? That's the place out on the highway next to the store, right?"

"Yes."

"I don't know, I'm going down to Key West this afternoon to do a little sightseeing. If I get back in time, I just might stop in. Thanks again ... Julie." Somehow her name felt good as it rolled off my tongue.

"Good bye, Sonny. I hope to see you tonight."

I may have told her that I *might* be stopping into Pa Bell's place for drink, but I knew darn well that I'd be there for sure.

After my initial meeting with Julie Albright, I walked around Wrecker's Key for a while. I strolled along the beach for maybe ten minutes, until it ended and the channel opened up to the expansive waters of Florida Bay and the Gulf of Mexico beyond that. Where the white sand ended, skirting an area thick with Brazilian Peppers and Red Mangroves, I took off my sneakers and sloshed my way through the muck of a tidal flat that had been exposed by a receding tide. After trekking through that stuff for maybe fifty yards, I stepped back onto dry land and saw something through a jungle of thick brush and trees. There was a house back in there.

The coolest, most rustic, two-story house I'd ever seen. It was built "Conch" style – that Bahamian and New England mixture of architecture that is so prevalent in the Florida Keys. I didn't know it at the time, but more than a hundred and fifty years earlier Thadeus Bell himself had built the home with boards he'd salvaged from a Bahamian wreck out near Looe Key one January morning during a blue nor'easter.

The home was the only permanent building on the

key, other than the one housing the little convenience store and bar out on US 1. A wide veranda encircled the entire place and the back of it faced a dock and the pristine waters of the bay. Two dormers were on either side of its large sloping roof, and a cupola was mounted on at its peak. The home was surrounded by a spotty, sun-parched lawn; the result of yet another soon-to-end, "dry season." In front of the place, beneath two huge Poinciana trees bursting with flaming-red flowers, there was an oversized bell resting on the lawn – an antique ship's bell made of solid brass. From where I stood I had to squint, but I could see that something had been written on it. The faded white letters that had been painted on it said, "The Bells."

Standing there, surrounded by the early morning calls being made by many strange, unseen birds *and* something rustling in the nearby palmettos, I felt like an intruder. And I did not like it. Pa Bell had seemed like a decent guy when I'd met him the day before, but nobody likes a relative stranger snooping around his place, Quickly but quietly, I headed back toward the water. This time winding my way through a different maze of trees, each and every one of them with Strangler Figs snaked around their trunks – robbing them of nourishment, slowly starving them.

When I finally reached the beach again, I paused after noticing two rippling circles on the glass-like surface of the water. The top halves of two tailfins were in the center of them thirty yards away, waving gently above the transparent water. That was all I could see with the wide, blue sky reflecting brightly on the surface, but I knew exactly what kind of fish they were. A pair of bonefish; the "gray ghosts" of the tropical flats, were foraging for crustaceans amongst the eel grass that carpeted the shallow water. That's why their tails had protruded from the surface. I'd read about them many times in fishing magazines. They are one of the most coveted game fish in the sport fishing world, and now that I was in the Keys I'd soon be getting a chance to fish for them. It's incomprehensible to an angler who has never hooked one of these speedsters, but a bonefish weighing just six or seven pounds can strip two-hundred yards line from a reel in one blazing run.

"Damn!" I whispered aloud, not wanting to spook the wary fish, "Why didn't I bring a light spinning outfit?"

But I wouldn't have had a chance even if I had brought a rod with me. Something out on the flat spooked the two bonefish. Maybe it was a leopard ray or a cruising shark, but either way both of the fish were gone in a flash. Surely they had headed to deeper, more protective water.

During the rest of the walk back to the trailer, my mind kept returning to Julie Albright. It seemed so unusual that such an attractive lady acted so sincere right from the beginning. I'd met my share of good-lookers and most of them seemed somewhat catty. I often got the impression that to them, toying with men was sport, just like fishing was to me. But this Julie was different. She seemed so genuine. When we had been only minutes into our conversation, I somehow felt as though I'd known her for years. I didn't have to play any roles. She'd made an impression on me for sure – an admirable one. But that was something I really wasn't ready for. Not as early on in the healing process as I was.

* * * * *

That afternoon I took my long-awaited drive down to Key West. It had been seventeen years since Wendy and I had gone to "the southernmost city" on our honeymoon. This time around I was returning alone. All I had with me were the conflicting, melancholic memories of happier times and those of my defeated marriage. I didn't know if this trip was going to bolster the bitterness I'd felt during the months since our breakup or supplant it with rekindled pain.

Only twenty minutes after leaving Wrecker's, I pulled into Key West on US 1 – the only road leading on or off the six-square-mile island. And as soon as I got there, what's the first thing I see? A Holiday Inn! Looking through the windshield the way I was, it was right smack in front of me – the very same motel where Wendy I spent five blissful days all those years ago.

"Oh, great," I muttered to myself, grinding my molars, shaking my head ever so slowly, "just what I need to see the minute I get here. This sure as hell isn't going to do anything to raise my spirits."

Fortunately, when I turned right onto North Roosevelt Boulevard, my mind was quickly drawn to something else. Standing just to my left, on a grassy median that separated the traffic lanes, was an obese, barefoot man dressed in dirty khaki shorts and nothing else. With dark lifeless eyes and hair hanging past his shoulders the unfortunate soul had layers of deeply tanned fat, drooping down from his sweaty paunch like a deflated truck tire. Obviously homeless, he was clutching a cardboard sign announcing that he'd work for food. Below that "Vietnam Vet" was spelled out.

After passing him I tried to envision how Key West might have looked more than fifty years earlier when Ernest Hemingway lived there. I'd always been fascinated by the Hemingway legend, reading everything about "the man" I could get my hands on. It didn't matter who wrote about him; Carlos Baker, Hem's ex-wives, his children, friends or anybody else, I would read it. My interest was that great, and now that I was actually back in Key West, I was heading directly to 907 Whitehead Street, the Hemingway home/museum.

Steering carefully down narrow, busy streets, I had to dodge all kinds of obstacles. There were colorfully-dressed pedestrians; tourists zipping around on pink mopeds, and locals on tired, old bicycles, peddling along as if they hadn't a care in the world. Turning the wheel this way and that I still managed glances at all the quaint Conch houses surrounding me. Some had cupolas on top of their roofs and most had handmade gingerbread trim.

Momentarily fixing my eyes on one of the old wooden structures, I recalled something I'd once read. The book said that many of these homes had actually been built in the Bahamas. They were brought to Key West in sections, by ship. Once they arrived their walls were reassembled – held together with the customary wooden pegs rather than nails.

In just a matter of minutes, I was standing by the double front doors of the Hemingway home, paying the admission fee along with a small group of camera-wielding tourists. Like a flock of ducklings trailing their mother, we went from room to room, first floor to second, obediently following and listening to our tour guide. A small, frail, older man with wide, red suspenders holding up his britches he was very knowledgeable and did a great job making our visit a truly enjoyable one. And wow, did he know a lot about the famous author who once lived there. At one point in the tour, when our guide was taking questions, I was tempted to ask him if he knew what size underwear Papa Hemingway wore. I was all but certain he could have told me. But I didn't ask. We were about two-thirds the way through the house when a dark funk suddenly drifted over my good spirits.

When we were leaving one bedroom to go to another I got the shock of my life. Standing at the very back of the group, I turned one last time to look at the two open doors leading out to a veranda. I remembered back to when I went there with Wendy, and she said how she absolutely loved them. How she would have given anything to spend just one night of our honeymoon in that room. Now, standing there, looking out at that veranda, I could have sworn I saw a vision of my ex-wife. Dressed in a floor-length white gown – looking more beautiful than ever – she was leaning with her lower back against the veranda's black, iron railing. She was looking directly at me, with that fantastic smile of hers.

Not believing what I was seeing, I turned my head and eyes to the side, squinted real hard then rolled my eyes to their corners, looking back over there. She was gone.

My heart started to pound. I swallowed hard then realized that all the hair on my arms was standing straight up.

Oh my god, what in the hell is wrong with me? I've got to get out of here – right now!

Without saying a word to anybody, I turned away and headed straight for the stairway. Quietly but quickly I made my way down the stairs and out the door.

Chapter 5

As soon as I stepped into the bright sunshine outside the Hemingway House, I realized I hadn't really seen Wendy in there. I wasn't that far gone yet. I told myself I was just tired – that all the stress and heartache since my birthday had weighed heavily on me. The long, three-day drive to Florida hadn't helped either, nor did the uncertainty of what my life would be like in the coming days, weeks and months.

I sat on a bench in the side yard for a while, resting my mind the best I could. After quickly convincing myself that fatigue was definitely my problem, I stayed there a while in the shade of a tall fig tree, watching the descendants of Hemingway's six-toed cat laze beneath bushes and out on the lawn. With no other visitors in this quiet part of the estate, time seemed to slow down and so did my thoughts. Things focused back into their proper perspective, and I was very thankful for that.

Later on I drove the short distance to Elizabeth Street, parked the van, and walked for a while amongst the legions of tourists scurrying up and down bustling Duval Street. It was there that I decided I still liked Key West. I knew I could live there if I found work and an affordable apartment, but the latter would *have* to be a little ways from Duval Street – on a quiet side street or lane. After knocking around for some time, I picked up copies of the Key West Citizen and the Keynoter, the local papers, and was fortunate enough to find a vacant bar stool at Sloppy Joe's. The place was jam-packed, but I had a pretty good time nursing a couple of cold Coronas, listening to the band and people watching. After a while I opened the newspapers and checked out the classified ads. The work situation did not seem very good and apartments were very expensive to rent. Somewhat disheartened, I took my last swallow of beer and left. The whole time I was there I hadn't once allowed myself to look at the table in a far corner where Wendy and I once sat.

While driving back to Wrecker's Key at dusk I, for the first time, questioned my decision to come to Florida. I had a troubling feeling that it may not have been the right thing to do. Steering my van across a small bridge between two uninhabited keys, I wondered about that as I looked out over the endless expanse of water. Way, way out there, on the western horizon, the huge magenta sun seemed to be melting into the Gulf of Mexico. It was a magnificent site, but it was also a blurry site. I was looking at it through misty eyes.

With my spirits low as they were, I had all but decided not to go to Barnacle Bell's that night. I was in no mood to be around a bunch of jovial holiday revelers. But all that changed when I drove onto Wrecker's Key at around nine o'clock. As I came up on the bar, I suddenly had one of those do-I-or-don't-I moments. The next thing I knew I found myself making a sharp left into its crushed-shell parking lot. As much as I didn't want to be around people right then, I wanted to be alone inside the trailer even less.

With the marl crunching beneath my tires, I actually had to look for a place to park. Cars and pickup trucks, most sporting Monroe County plates, were lined up door to door in front and on both sides of the wooden building. Barnacle Bell's was not your basic tourist oasis. Most of the vehicles belonged to locals from nearby Big Pine and Summerland Keys. I found a place to park, stepped out into the balmy evening air, and inhaled deeply. I didn't know if I really wanted to go inside, but with the thick ocean air now filling my lungs and the perfume-like scent of night blooming jasmine in the air, I ambled slowly towards the front door of Barnacle Bell's.

Inside, patrons were shoulders to elbows around the circular mahogany bar, some sitting on stools, still more standing. Somebody dropped a cell phone on the floor and when I glanced down at it I noticed that around the bar's base a rigid anchor chain had been fashioned into a footrest. The place was saturated with barroom chatter. Pa Bell, wearing a long, white apron like that of a butcher, was at the center of this arena, methodically mixing drinks. All along the bar there were sweating, brown and clear beer bottles and all sorts of pink and yellow libations adorned with tiny pastel umbrellas. Despite the efforts of two, seemingly-tired paddle fans, a thin cloud of smoke remained intact just beneath the ceiling. On the back wall, next to a flashing blue "Coors" sign, a huge tiger shark jaw hung. Its gaping mouth was frozen open, exposing seven rows of ferocious, triangular teeth. To the side of a small cleared area for dancing, a hippie-like duet – a man and woman both with long hair parted in the middle and matching paisley bellbottoms, strummed guitars as they sung the lyrics to Creedence Clearwater Revival's classic hit *Bad Moon Rising*.

I wasn't standing there for very long when, in the dim light, Julie Albright suddenly appeared like a beautiful apparition. She'd been sitting in a back corner talking with three men, and I couldn't help but suspect she'd been keeping an eye on the bar's entrance. I say that because I hadn't been standing there but a few seconds when she quickly rose from her chair and started making her way toward me. As she slid between two couples, each of them grinding away on the makeshift dance floor, Julie looked more intoxicating than straight tequila. She was wearing snug, white jeans and a black halter-top that really enhanced the fullness of her breasts. The white hoops that danced beneath her ears as she strode in my direction contrasted beautifully with her flowing raven hair. She was totally female alright – the rare kind of women that could turn the head of a celibate monk.

Funny thing was, even though her smile was wide when she came up to me, she seemed a tad shy. I couldn't help it, but she put me to mind of a smitten schoolgirl when she said, "I'm glad you could make it, Sonny. Did you have a good time in Key West?"

"A real trip!" I said in a tongue-in-cheek tone before quickly catching myself. "Yes ... it was nice down there, kind of like a tropical Greenwich Village."

"That's one fitting analogy if I ever heard one," she said, taking my hand.

All of a sudden I thought *she* might not have been all that bashful after all. With my hand now in hers – tight as she was holding it – I was the one feeling embarrassed. Just like an adrenaline rush does, an arousing flood of heat suddenly coursed through my entire body. Now *I* was the one feeling like a school kid, and I didn't like it. I was just about to give myself a mental lambasting but before I could Julie said, "Come with me. I want you to meet some of the locals." Still hand in hand, feeling as if she were a teacher and I a student in tow, she led me to a wooden table where the three men sat.

"Guys, this is Sonny Raines. He just came down from Long Island, and he'll be staying in Mr. Doyle's trailer for a few days. "Sonny, this is Jack, Buster, and Fred."

As I shook hands with them they all seemed friendly enough. When I stretched my arm across the table to shake Jack's hand, I noticed that he was sitting in a wheelchair. After that I settled into the empty seat next to Julie.

"What part of Long Island you from?" the stocky, red-headed Jack Beers asked.

"I grew up in Queens ... but I've been out in Smithtown for about 15 years."

"Jack's an ex-Brooklyn policeman," Julie interjected; obviously intent on making this meeting go smoothly.

I was about to glance at the wheelchair again but caught myself and said, "This is a long way from Brooklyn, how do you like it down here?"

"This is as close to heaven as I've ever been ... right here on Wreckers Key. Ain't no other place for me," Jack said, his neck seemingly having a tough time supporting his slightly bobbing and wavering head. I wondered if he had some kind of physical impairment or if he was just lubed-up from too much beer. There were quite a few empty bottles on the table.

A moment later the astute-looking, bald guy, Fred Sampson, turned to the ex-cop and said, "Yeah, you were just what we needed here, Beers, another New

Yorker."

"Okay," Jack came back, "lighten up there plowboy. Otherwise I might just run you over with my chair."

Fred Sampson only smiled. It was obvious the two men were good friends. Fred then turned to me asking, "How are things up north ... the economy picking up at all?"

"Nope, it's getting worse all the time."

"I hear you," Fred Sampson came back, as if we were both on the same page. He then laid the cigar he'd been holding in an ashtray, straightened up in his chair a bit, downed a shot of whiskey in one motion and continued, "I used to be a pretty a well-paid economist for a big company up in Indianapolis, until I dropped out. Had my fill of the bullshit corporate scene, came down here eight years ago, and never once looked back. Yupper, I'm like Jack – perfectly content being right here."

As I was talking to the two men, I could feel Julie's alluring eyes locked onto me. Out of the periphery of my own, I'd been watching her. And now she turned her head to the bar. Pa Bell was hustling his tail off behind it when Julie said, "Pa should have asked Sissy to help out tonight. He's having one heck of a time pouring drinks and serving them to the people at tables, too. I'll go get ours." Standing up now she asked, "How about it, anybody for another drink? Sonny, what will you have?"

After I asked for a Miller Lite and everybody else requested refills, Julie went to the bar, stepped behind it, and got the drinks herself. As she did, all but the most preoccupied male eyes around the noisy circular bar were watching her every move. She was that gorgeous. Even the women sitting on stools watched her, throwing daggers from their jealous eyes. Once Julie returned with all the libations atop a round metal tray, she handed me mine first, and as I thanked her I just had to steal another brief, assessing look. I'd always had a thing for women with long hair; especially long black hair.

I wasn't the only person that night who thought Julie was giving most of her attention to me. When she slipped away to the ladies room later on Buster Bell said to me in his slow easy way, "Ya know ... Julie seems to be takin' a particular likin' to you."

Taken off guard, not knowing what to say, I just looked at him for a quick moment. A big strapping man in his mid-forties, he was wearing a red ball cap with a "Red Man" patch on its crown. By this time he, like the other men, was a few drinks deep, and the cap was tilted way back on his head. The long, sun-bleached hair that hung down in waves from beneath it touched his shoulders and framed a large blocky face. But it was a boyish face, an amiable face.

"Oh, I don't know," I said, dropping my eyes to the beer bottle on the table in front of me then turning it a bit. "I just think she's being nice because I'm new down here."

"Believe me," Buster came back, "I've known Julie for quite a spell now, and I ain't never seen her get all goo-goo-eyed like she is tonight."

"Come on, man," I said, "she's just being hospitable."

"Hospitable my ass," Jack Beers chimed in, his voice slightly slurred. "Julie's got her eye on you, my friend. You're one lucky guy. I can't tell you how many men I've seen hit on her and get nowhere. She's a true lady and a class act."

I kept to myself the fact that I was still trying to get over the loss of my wife. I also didn't mention, even after a few beers, that my mind had drifted back to Wendy more than once during our conversation. And I of course didn't say a word about how I tried to picture Wendy sitting in Julie's empty seat when she had first gotten up to get the drinks. On the other hand, I couldn't help but feel very fortunate that the three men thought I'd been the object of Julie's attention all evening. I liked that it did seem quite obvious. But then again, there was that lesson I'd learned early in life. The one I picked up firsthand during my adolescence – a man can *never* take anything for granted when he's around a woman he doesn't know too well. There is no way he can be totally sure he knows what's going on in her mind – not until she comes right out and says it. *Nooo,* I thought to myself, *that's just her way! She's nice to everybody.*

But I was wrong. About the time I was getting ready to call it a night, head back to the trailer, something happened. Something convinced me that the way Julie had been acting was far more than just her innate good-natured personality.

During the entire hour and a half I'd been at Barnacle Bell's she had only drank one glass of red wine. Another was sitting on the table in front of her by now, but she'd been nursing it for quite some time. Since she hadn't drank much I knew well and good that while Fred, Buster and Jack were deep into a discussion about the Miami Dolphins the private, alluring smile that rose on Julie's lips had nothing to do with alcohol. Neither did the telltale look in her eyes – her *bedroom* eyes. As our eyes locked together, the sixties-throwback duet had just begun a rendition of the old Bee Gees hit *To Love Somebody.* It's a slow song, an emotional one, and as soon as Julie heard it she laid her hand on top of my thigh. Her smile widened in a way I can best describe as adoringly, and she whispered in my ear, "Come on, Sonny. Dance with me."

Our gaze lingered for just a moment before I stubbed out my eighth cigarette of the day and found myself saying, "Sure ... why not?"

As if *I* were some kind of prize, Julie led me by the hand through the crowd. Once we were out on the dance floor, she quickly but gently slid her hands around the small of my back, drawing me toward her. The feeling was incredible; the scent of her perfume, my face nestled against hers, the slight tickle of her ebony hair, the heat from her uplifted breasts and stomach snug against my body. As our hips slowly swayed in unison I felt like I was going to implode. Then she held me tighter yet, and together we listened to the music and the old song's sentimental lyrics.

As we danced on, something told me that Julie Albright was overwhelmed by desires she hadn't felt in a long, long time. I can't tell you why, but I just knew it. And I was right. Just before the song ended she whispered something in my ear. Her voice was low and sensual, but I couldn't quite discern her words. Leaning my head back, I asked her what she'd said. She didn't answer right away. Instead she studied my face, as if she was double-checking something. Then her eyes shifted to mine. She looked at them – into them, for what seemed like a long time but really wasn't. It was one of those moments when time seemed to stand still. Finally she spoke. In that same soft, sexy tone she said, "Come home with me, Sonny. Let's go right now."

We said good bye to the guys at the table, paid the tab then drove in the darkness back through the pines to Julie's trailer.

As I followed her, I saw in the periphery of my headlights a raccoon coming out of the woods. It stepped quickly to the side of the road, reared up on its hind legs, and looked my way. It was uncanny. In the conical light the black-masked animal's eyes glowed bright yellow, and they seemed to be looking into the van – directly at me. The creature stared through the windshield, right into my eyes. I didn't know why but I immediately thought of Wendy. "No!" I said shaking my head. "Don't be ridiculous." I of course didn't believe it was a sign or a message or anything hokey like that, but Wendy did appear in my mind. And when I saw her face, I suddenly believed there was no way I'd going inside Julie's trailer with her. Quickly, frantically, I started scouring my mind for an excuse.

A minute or so later Julie pulled in alongside her place and I parked next to Doyle's. I knew by then what I was going to tell her – the truth. That deep inside, angry as I was with my ex-wife, I still hoped we'd somehow get back together. But I didn't tell Julie that. As I stepped across the thin strip of grass separating the two aluminum trailers, my plan went all to hell. For standing outside her car now, in the soft light of the moon, Julie Albright looked like Venus herself. Not only did the glow from the heavens accentuate every curve of her body, but it highlighted all the kind, beautiful features on her face. I was mesmerized. I'd have followed her anywhere.

When I walked around her car and stood in front of her she took my hand. I'll never forget the way that moon reflected in her eyes when she looked up at me and said, "Sonny, I don't want you to think I'm a fast woman. It's been quite some time since ... since I've been with a man. And when I'm around you, well, I get these feelings. Good feelings, undeniable feelings, feelings that I've only felt one other time in my life."

She rose to her toes then and kissed my lips gently before saying, "Come with me."

And I did.

Hand in hand, we walked through the screened porch, went inside, and made our way to a small bedroom in the back of her home. After Julie switched on a small bedside lamp, she fused her dark, alluring eyes to mine. She kept them there as she slipped off her halter top and undid the front of her bra. That was it. No longer did anybody or anything else exist. It was all Julie and me. I could no longer hear the crickets outside. There was no Wendy, no Steve Silverman, no Ronald Halstead, or any nagging concerns about my future. It was just the two of us, the here and now, and our carnal instincts. At first we explored each other's bodies – gently searching, touching, and caressing as we kissed. But the prelude didn't last long. Soon our anticipation and urges became uncontrollable. Urgently, as if the trailer was on fire and there wasn't much time, Julie took me and we became one. Flooded by pleasure as we were, our minds no longer seemed to belong to us. There was no thinking. We only did what came natural. Desperately, recklessly, our muscles tightening and bodies shuddering, we made passionate love until finally, simultaneously, we climaxed. In all the years Wendy and I had been together I'd never experienced anything like this. And when it was over, Julie Albright and I slept well together. We were two mates; satisfied, relaxed, so thankful to have found each other.

The next morning I woke an hour after the sun's first rays crept through the vertical blinds. Back in the trees, behind the trailer, the two mocking birds were making a ruckus as they ceaselessly squawked at each other. A blue jay called, "Jay, jay, jay," from a place deeper in the woods, and I turned my head to look at Julie lying beside me. Her naked, flawless body was in the fetal position, a pillow clutched snugly to her white breasts. I studied her, and I couldn't believe how fortunate I'd been to have found her. But my sense of deep contentment didn't last. Something happened. I noticed something – something very, very unsettling.

Julie's left hand was exposed, just above her pillow, and I was shocked by what I saw. No, I was devastated. There were only three full fingers on her hand. Half of her pinky was missing and all of her ring finger. My face went slack and my lower jaw dropped. All I could do was gawk at her. I felt as if I'd been cheated, as if something too wonderful for words had been stolen from me. As she had sensed my gaze, Julie slowly opened her eyes. She saw my eyes trained on that hand, and the shock on my face. Without lifting her head from the pillow, her eyes pivoted to her lost fingers. Ever so slowly, she closed her hand.

My eyes then came up to hers, and I didn't have a clue what to say. I tried in vain to speak, but nothing would come out. What could possibly be appropriate in a situation such as this? Both of us in deep, disappointed thought, Julie continued to look at me and me at her. She was crushed. Finally, unable to counterfeit a smile, she asked, "Should I put some coffee on?" She knew what my answer would be. That strong connection we'd felt since the moment we'd met the morning before just wasn't there anymore. Poof! As if it had been short-circuited it was gone.

"No, that's o.k." I said as nonchalantly as possible. "I ... I haven't had any exercise for over a week. I want to jog a few miles before it gets too hot outside." Then, while rising from the bed I added, "When I run, I have to do it first thing or I won't do it at all."

She said nothing else. She only laid there as I dressed in the quiet. I was disappointed all right, but I was at odds with myself and embarrassed as well. Never had I been in such an awkward situation. I felt like an A-1 heel for not staying to have a cup of coffee with her, but I couldn't. I *had* to get out of there. All I wanted to do was bolt.

When I was finally dressed I looked down at Julie Albright and said in as earnest a voice as I could muster, "Thanks for having me over. I'll probably see you later."

Then I walked out of the trailer.

Chapter 6

As soon as I stepped outside I broke into a trot. Passing all the rest of the trailers first then heading up the same narrow road I followed Julie home on the night before, all I could do was think about how she must be reacting right then. I envisioned her staying in her bed alone, thinking. I could see quiet tears making their way down her cheeks. We may have only known each other for twenty-four hours but the mutual attraction we felt – both mental and physical, was undeniable. And it was deep. I knew for sure she really liked me, but there was a lot I didn't know about Julie Alright.

I had no idea she hadn't had a semblance of interest in any man since her modeling days ended sixteen years earlier in New York City. Nor did I know that back then she was engaged to Mark Richardson, a very promising young attorney. Mark was about to become the youngest partner ever at Dalrymple, Stockton and Stockton, one of New York's most prestigious law firms. Julie and Mark had been dating for two years, and they had a big wedding planned for that fall. The ceremony was to be held in St. Patrick's Cathedral, followed by a reception at the Waldorf Astoria. Money was no problem for Mark's parents and they insisted on buying the grandest wedding available. His father, J. Walter Richardson of Scarsdale and Palm Beach, just happened to be the sole heir of the "American Grains" breakfast cereal fortune.

At that time Julie was one of the big up-and-comers in the modeling world. As a matter of fact, she was just about to cross the threshold to cover-girl fame. But it never happened. One June morning, when she was on her way to the biggest shoot of her career, her sunny future eclipsed totally, and in an instant.

Sitting in the back seat of a Checker cab, she was headed uptown to the world-renowned Clairidge Studios where she was to pose for an upcoming cover of *Vogue Magazine*. The sun was beginning to shine, but Madison Avenue was still slick from a late morning rain. Julie, who was sitting behind the driver, cranked down the window and held her left hand out in the breeze, drying her freshly applied nail polish. Then, just as the cab was crossing the intersection at 44th street, another cab, heading east, didn't bother to stop for the red light. The driver of the at fault cab, one Eloi Hernandez, was so toasted on coke he didn't even notice the light had turned red. Thoughts of stopping never entered his hopped-up mind until after he'd sped into the intersection – and slammed broadside into Julie's cab. The impact to the driver's door was so forceful that her driver's neck snapped so far sideways it literally cracked. The two vehicles then skidded, smacking sideways into each other, crushing four of Julie's fingers in the process.

The driver of Julie's cab, a Greek immigrant from

Astoria Queens, whose name she never learned, was dead by the time the ambulances reached the scene. Julie was rushed to Mt. Sinai Hospital where a team of three plastic surgeons performed micro-surgery in an attempt to re-attach her fingers. Her middle and index fingers were salvaged and the nerves regenerated in due time, but her pinky and ring finger were so badly mashed there was no possible way of saving them. Eloi Hernandez did a short stint on Riker's Island; the Greek was buried out in Queens by his family; and Julie's potential international fame never materialized. On top of all that, when Mark Richardson found out Julie had lost two fingers, he decided that just maybe he wasn't ready for marriage after all. After knotting the loose ends of her life together the best Julie could, she returned to Ft. Lauderdale with lost dreams and a broken heart.

I was panting heavily as I jogged past the side of Pa Bell's store and headed north on U.S. 1. Moving at a good clip by now, the palmettos and Florida Holly alongside the early-morning-quiet two-lane highway blurred green in my periphery. I pushed hard, lengthening my strides – punishing myself. Nagging thoughts about what happened ten minutes earlier whirred in and out of my head so quickly that I could only hold onto a few. But they were enough. I went back and forth, condoning and lambasting myself for the way I'd just acted around Julie. I was so sorry she'd seen that dumb stare on my face after noticing her handicap, but I couldn't help it. And sure, Julie was beautiful, kind, smart and more, but she *was* handicapped too. Over and over, as if trading punches, the two sides of my conscious mind parried each other.

Hell man, what's wrong with you! Can't you see she's a very special woman? Yeah, maybe so, but I could never get over the hand thing. It would be always be there, like an eternal dark asterisk, always taking away from the rest of her. Maybe so, but look at the rest of her. Look at what a kind human being she is. I know, I know, but I could never accept the fingers thing. I'm better off not getting in any deeper with her. You think so, huh! Think about ... .

On and on I went like that until I finally slowed from a jog to an easy trot. As I cooled down the best I could with the morning sun hot on my perspiring back, I finally decided the last thing I needed was to get into some kind of stressful relationship.

"That's it," I said aloud, by now slowing to a walk on the marl road back toward the trailer park, "I don't want to think about it anymore. Even if she did have all her fingers, I'm not ready to get mixed up with another woman so soon. Hell, I'm not even over my broken marriage yet ... probably never will be."

Before reaching the trailers I came upon another road that cut into the pines on the left. Even narrower than the one I was on, I'd seen it before and suspected it led to Pa Bell's place. I needed to talk to him, and rather than walk to the beach then wade the shallows around the mangroves again I turned up that road. I didn't feel like talking to anybody, but I *had* to talk to the old man. After checking the rents for apartments in the papers at Sloppy Joe's the day before, I'd finally admitted to myself that, without a job, I couldn't possibly afford a place in Key West yet. As much as I did not want to be next door to Julie anymore, I had no choice. With not a whole lot of money behind me, the deal Pa Bell was giving me was just too sweet to walk away from.

Just before I reached Pa's house, the slash pines gave way to tall gumbo limbo trees and stately banyans with trunks wide across as a man is tall. High above, a dense ceiling of motionless leaves hid the birds whose calls and songs filled this forest. It was as if I were in a wide, verdant, majestic tunnel. As if I had stepped into a place that was half jungle and half rain forest. When most people think of heaven they envision a place with fluffy white clouds and an endless blue sky, but this green Eden was the closest to the Promised Land I could ever imagine. Everywhere I looked there were bushes, shrubs, clusters of flowers, long vines hanging from tree limbs. Yes, the place was absolutely breathtaking. And as I walked on I couldn't help but feel I was previewing that eternal, peaceful sanctuary that's promised us by so many religions.

By the time I made my way to Pa Bell's front

lawn the towering canopy had thinned some, but I was still shrouded in shade. A well-worn footpath cut across the grass to the front of the house and after I stepped onto it I just stood there for a moment. From where I was standing the first time I'd seen Pa's place, I hadn't seen through the dense bush the two massive Poinciana trees now standing before me. Like towering twin sentinels, their long limbs intertwined above the path, forming yet another tunnel. But this one was different. A person would have to travel this world far and wide to witness a sight more magnificent than a Royal Poinciana in full bloom. And here I was, looking up at two. With the expansive boughs of these trees bursting with vibrant, flaming-red flowers above me, I knew I was looking up at some of Mother Nature's finest work. I walked beneath them with my head tilted way back, still marveling with every step. But at the same time, a feeling other than wonderment came over me. I became somewhat leery. I didn't know what to expect. Not knowing Pa Bell very well I felt like I was crossing a border into his private world. And I was.

After slowly climbing the wide wooden steps to the veranda, gently I rapped the door with the brass door knocker – a miniature ship's bell with the family name "Bell" inscribed in it.

Nobody answered. I knocked again, still no answer.

I walked around the side of the house, skirted an

old brick cistern then saw the old man. He was standing on a narrow wooden dock, facing Florida Bay, leaning over the railing at the end of it with his back to me. Not wanting to startle him, I announced my presence by walking heavily on the faded gray planking. As I approached he turned around.

"Hello, Mister Bell."

Calmly as can be, as if he'd already known I was on his property, he said, "Mornin'." Then he looked into a white plastic bucket sitting next to him on the dock, reached in, grabbed a handful of small dead fish and flipped them over the railing. I came up alongside him and we both looked down into the clear water. I couldn't believe what I was seeing.

All at once an entire school of ten to fifteen-pound snook rushed for the baitfish. As they struck the slowly sinking cigar minnows, sunlight reflected in bright flashes off their silvery sides. One of the small fish floated on the surface but it wasn't long before a large snook crashed it. Its huge mouth agape, water flew everywhere and it produced a loud, distinct popping sound.

Pa then repeated the process, and with my eyes still glued to the water I said, "Wow, this is something else. They're all nice size fish."

"See that one over there, the one laying in the eel grass?" Pa asked, pointing a sausage-like finger toward the far edge of the school, "Been feeding him for years. Call him 'Old Moe'."

"How do you know it's the same fish?"

"That's easy," Pa answered, squinting into the sunlight, "see that there scar at the base of his tail ... where his black lateral line ends?"

"Ohhh yeah," I said, studying the fish like an ichthyologist.

"Well ... when Buster found 'im he was still runnin' gill nets, right out there at the front of this channel. Anyway, this one time he pulled up the net and Old Moe was stuck in it, by his tail. Where that scar is he had a diver's spear plum through his body. It got tangled in the mesh."

Pa lit up a Lucky Strike then and I thought about having my first smoke of the day. But I didn't. I wanted to hold off until I had my morning coffee.

Exhaling as he spoke Pa said, "Buster put 'im in the live well and brought him here to the dock. We sawed the spear in half, pulled it out, and let 'im go."

"And he's still here."

"Yep! He's still hangin' 'round the dock. Snook favor stayin' around structures you know."

It was easy to see that this man loved to talk about

the sea and the life it sustains. That became even more obvious as he went on with his story.

"One evenin' at dusk I was cullin' the dead mullet out of the live well aboard the 'Island Belle' – that's our old Chris-Craft cabin cruiser ... Buster's out in it right now. Anyway, after I flipped the first mullet over the side I heard a pop. I looked down there and saw 'Old Moe' layin' there, motionless; eyeballin' me. I threw him another one and this time saw him grab it. Been feedin' him and his brood ever since."

With my eyebrows now arched much the way Pa's were permanently, I said, "I'd say that's really getting in touch with nature."

"Nowadays it's a lot easier than connectin' with most people."

"Yeah," I said, looking out at Wreckers Channel now, "people are so busy running around in a frenzy today most of them don't have time for each other anymore."

"That's part of the beauty of this here key. There ain't many of us and nobody's ever in a rush. We have plenty of time to be neighborly. Been that way since my great-grand-daddy came here to Wrecker's Key in the 1830's. He was the first white man to settle here."

"Interesting! So your family's been here ever since?"

"Yup, only difference, 'cept for a little increase in boat traffic, is all those tourists rushin' by out on U.S. 1. Let me tell ya, there's some real characters pass through here. Hell, just last weekend we had some first-class bozos from Miami stop at the store. They were all liquored-up and wanted ta fill the boat they were trailerin' with gas. One of them put the nozzle into a rod-holder instead of the fuel fill and poured eighty dollars worth of regular onto the floor of the boat!

"Haaa! Some kind of characters they must have been!"

As we shared a good laugh, a brown pelican landed next to Pa on the dock. He called him "Max" then hand fed him a fish and stroked his white head a couple of times. The bird was perfectly fine with this show of affection, but when I leaned to take a look at him he took one cumbersome step back.

"Mister Bell," I said then, in a more serious tone, "the reason why I came over here was to ask you if there's any possibility I could rent Mr. Doyle's Airstream for a little longer. I mean ... unless he's coming back soon?"

Pa pursed his lips in thought and said, "Son, I wish he was comin' back. He was a good friend and was here a long time, but I'm afraid it'd take one of them miracles to bring him back from where he is now."

"Oh, I see. I'm sorry to hear that."

Thinking of his lost friend now, Pa suddenly lost his kind, even-tempered demeanor. In just a flash the sadness in his old eyes turned to anger.

"Godamned developers down in the Saddlebunch Keys *killed* him, just like they kill everything else – for the quick money. Ole Doyle was waitin' to pull out onto U.S. 1, out front of my store, when a flatbed flies by. This guy's haulin' three big sable palms to some new condo down on Saddlebunch, and he loses one, wasn't tied down snug. It landed smack on top of the hood of Doyle's old pickup ... rolled with such force that it smashed into the windshield and crushed him. He was killed instantly." Shaking his head in disgust now, his eyelids beginning to tremble, Pa said, "Them useless Chamber of Commerce types ... politicians, developers, investors, all of 'em. They're more venomous than a pissed-off cottonmouth, when it comes to money. No matter how much they got, it ain't never enough. They got no respect for nothin' or nobody!"

Seeing him this enraged made me a little nervous. It was obvious his resentment towards the developers and their cronies had been festering for a long, long time.

"Anyway," Pa continued, trying to compose himself now, "the firemen cut the cab open and the EMTs carted Doyle off to the morgue down in Key

West. To them developers, he wasn't nothin' more than a road kill. Just some old nobody, with no family anywhere to sue 'em."

"I'm really sorry, Mr. Bell."

There was a moment of uncomfortable silence before he finally asked, "You want to rent it month to month ... the trailer?"

"Sure. That would be fine."

"Hunert-and-fifty a month, plus electric and water."

"Sounds fair to me," I said, knowing better than to offer to pay up front.

"No fishing from the dock."

"Mister. Bell, I love to fish, but I'm a sportsman. I think you and I share a common respect for wildlife."

Looking directly into my eyes, Pa nodded slowly then. Knowing now that deal was done, I waited just a moment before saying, "I've got to get going now. I want to pick up some groceries over at the store."

"Sure. Okay. Tell Sissy I said to give you twenty percent off like I do all the others in the park." Then his wise eyes narrowed as if they were being pinched together and he said in a slightly deeper tone, "Be nice to Julie, now. She's one hell of a gal. It was plain to see last night that she's takin' a liking to you. I ain't never seen her act that interested in any man."

Just what I *didn't* need to hear. I did not need any additional pressure right then, but I knew Pa hadn't intended to tax my emotions. After all, he couldn't have known I went into Julie's trailer with her the night before. Or could he? Did he? Something in those alert, knowing eyes of his made me wonder.

Chapter 7

Most of us have a secret closet where we store all kinds of different masks. Depending on the people we encounter or the situations we find ourselves in, we can change our disguises in an instant. For that reason it can sometimes be harder to read people than to decipher ancient literature. But that wasn't the way it was with Sissy when I went to Pa's store to buy groceries that morning.

From the moment I stepped onto that worn, wooden floor, I knew something was up with her. She acted differently to the first time I was in there. Immediately, I could tell she was giving me the silent treatment. She must have somehow figured out what happened between me and her close friend, either that or Julie told her. No matter what, I did not like it. Just minutes earlier Pa had made me feel uncomfortable enough telling me to treat Julie right, now here was Sissy copping an attitude. With nobody else in the store as I perused the shelves, I tried twice to start a lighthearted conversation. I still got nothing. That was it. I didn't say another word. Not even when I went to pay Sissy. I was so angry that I didn't even mention the discount Pa told me to ask for.

After lugging a twelve-pack of beer and four bags of groceries to the trailer – kicking dust up in front of me most of the way, I decided I *had* to get all the clutter out of my head. I *needed* to go fishing. So after taking a quick shower in the phone-booth-size stall, loading my tackle box, bait bucket, and two rods into the van, I headed up to Big Pine Key to get some bait.

It was a good decision. In no time at all my negative thoughts simply vanished. How could they not? As I motored north there was a magnificent expanse of ocean on either side of me. On the right, way, way out in the Atlantic, I could see the dark blue waters of the Gulfstream. In closer, the shoals were a beautiful shade of turquoise and, closer yet, the water became a soothing mint green, mottled with dark patches where the shallow was coated with eel grass. Shimmering beneath an endless blue sky, this was a vision that could never be duplicated on any picture postcard.

As soon as I came off the bridge over Pine Channel onto Big Pine Key, I saw for the first time a diminutive Key deer. Driving through here last Friday, on my way south, I had seen numerous caution signs along the road advising to watch for the endangered deer, but I hadn't see any. Now, coming out of the sun-blanched palmettos alongside the road, there was a fully grown doe, maybe 30 inches high, and her tiny fawn. With no cars close behind me I slowed considerably, admiring the beauty of the docile animals. When I went by them they popped their heads up from the grass they were foraging and studied me with their shiny black Bambi eyes.

About a mile later I came upon a small block building with a huge red and white sign on its roof that screamed "BAIT". After swinging into the small parking area I pulled alongside a Chevy blazer with a "Save the reef" sticker on its rear bumper; killed the ignition and walked to the front door. Right in front of my nose there was a "Help Wanted" sign taped to the glass. "Hmmm," I muttered to myself as I leaned on the door and stepped inside.

The damp air in the store was laden with the smell of sea water from a shrimp tank and a touch of fresh mullet – one of the world's most exciting fragrances to a salty angler. Two men were talking in the rear of the well-stocked shop, almost surely about fishing. One was a tall, husky, bearded guy with a green "Penn" cap atop his blocky head, the other, about half his size, was rail-thin and sported the kind of dangerously dark suntan you can only get from too many hours on the water. The little guy sitting behind a glass display counter crammed full of reels was wearing khaki shorts and a khaki shirt – the unofficial uniform of Florida Keys charter boat captains. As I got closer I could read the "Cap Forest" embroidered over his breast pocket. Both men were gulping coffee from foam cups and smoking cigarettes. Neither looked my way so I figured they either hadn't noticed me or simply didn't give a damn. I couldn't help feeling like a no-count intruder as I walked around picking up some sinkers, hooks swivels and a bait bucket. It was only when I set my selections on top of the glass display case that they seemed to notice me.

"Lo," Cap Forest finally looked up and said. His deep-set eyes resembled road maps with all the red lines in them going north, east, south, and west.

"How're you doing?" I came back. "I need two dozen shrimp also."

"Help yourself to some coffee," Cap said, nodding at the Mr. Coffee machine on the end of the on counter.

"I think I will. Let me have three or four fresh mullet too, if you have them."

As I poured the steamy-hot brew into a cup the bigger man with the graying beard asked, "Where ya gonna fish?"

"Oh ... I'm just going over to the Wrecker's Hey Bridge to see if I can get a few snapper for dinner."

"You new here, or just on vacation?" he asked glancing out the front window at my New York plates.

"I'm *planning* on staying awhile. As a matter of fact, I wanted to ask about the job."

"What job?"

"Well, I saw the sign on the door when I came in."

"Oh yeahhh," he said, turning toward the captain

as he returned with my bucket of shrimp and four good sized mullet wrapped in newspaper.

"This here feller wants to know about the job, Cap."

I didn't think Forest had noticed my license plates but was pretty sure he did notice my accent. Knowing all too well that most people beyond the George Washington Bridge have no great love for New Yorkers, I figured he'd quickly blow me off.

"Where do ya live?"

"Bell's Trailer Park. Down on Wreckers Key."

"How long you been there?"

"As I was just telling this fella, I've only been here a few days. But I plan on staying,"

"Sorry, but I'm really lookin' for somebody who's been here awhile ... someone who knows about fishin' these parts."

"I realize that I'd have a lot to learn about your methods and fish, but I'm a quick learner. Up in Long Island, I've fished offshore for Mako shark, trolled, surf fished, and bottom fished too. I can rig baits, wrap rods, fix reels – the whole nine yards."

I could feel my sales instincts kicking in. I was selling myself the same way I'd sold hundreds of sofas in the past, and it seemed I might be turning things around now. Cap extracted another Doral cigarette from his pocket and tapped the unfiltered end over and over on the counter, as if he were considering me. Knowing that timing means everything in sales, I moved in for the close.

"I was going to look for work in Key West, but I'd love to work in a more relaxed atmosphere. I like things quiet."

Cap Forest ran a twitching hand back through his oily black hair one time then eyeballed me for a few seconds.

"You know what? You seem like a pretty sharp guy. I just might be able to give you a shot. But the job's only gonna pay eight an hour ... under the table."

I knew it would pay peanuts. But that was okay, I didn't know how long I was going to last in the Keys. There was a good chance I'd end up going back to New York. For the time being I could get by on the ridiculous salary, especially with the sweet deal Pa was giving me on the trailer. If things became tight, I could always take a few dollars from the money I'd brought with me.

"That's okay," I said, feeling my mouth pull into a small smile, "a guy's got to start somewhere, right?"

"Okay, I'll give you a try. I'll need you to work

Saturdays to Tuesdays, seven till five. That's only four days, but it'll come out to 40 hours. My wife, Maggie, she works the other days and the three evenings we stay open. You can start day after tomorrow. I'll work with you for two days, but after that I've got charters the rest of the week. You'll be on your own."

He extended his hand then and when I reached for it I couldn't help noticing all the fresh thin cuts on the heel of it, and on the outside of his pinky. I knew he'd gotten them from breaking monofilament.

"Name's Forest, but everyone calls me Cap," he said as we shook.

"Sonny, Sonny Raines."

Cap then looked at the other man and said, "This here's Dalton Judge. You'll be seein' him around here plenty. Can't seem ta keep him the hell away. Who knows? Maybe you can," Cap actually smiled for the first time.

"Okay, I'll see what I can do. Thanks! Thanks a lot. I'll see you in the A.M. I've got to go put a hurting on some of those snapper now."

After I paid for the fishing tackle and was making my way toward the door, Cap said from behind me, "Say hello ta Pa Bell for me. Haven't seen him in a month a Sundays."

I promised I would and when I reached to door Dalton Judge blurted in his husky voice, “Fish the fourth set of pilings on the south end of the bridge ... on the bay side.”

“Thanks for the tip. I’ll give it a try.”

I did fish that fourth set of pilings. And even though the tide was running out, I managed to get a few nice mangrove snappers for the pan. Content with my catch, I was walking off the bridge when a white pickup truck with a Monroe County logo on its door pulled behind my van where I’d parked on the Flagler’s Key side. Then a black Mercedes 560SL with dark shaded windows parked behind the truck. Just before the luxury car became obscured by the pickup though, I’d caught a glimpse of the vanity plate on its front bumper. It said WATERFRONT.

Two county workers in drab uniforms got out of the truck, and a tall, lean, middle-aged man, wearing what appeared to be a tailor-made white linen suit, got out of the Benz as if he were a conqueror climbing out of his chariot. As he strode alongside the road toward the pickup truck, I saw him looking at me. Once he reached the front of the truck he shifted his eyes to the New York plate on my old van, and he took one last glance my way. Probably thinking I was just another nickel-and-dime tourist, he then joined the two workers who were huddled over a sheet of paper one was holding. Quickly, as if the whole procedure were being timed by a stopwatch, one yanked a sign out of the back of the truck, and the three then double-timed it down a steep incline to the water. By the time I approached my van the workers were digging a hole by the shoreline – right smack in front of a dense group of mangrove trees – federally protected mangrove trees. The suit, who watched them closely, was holding the sign now.

I stole a few more peeks as I slowly loaded my fishing rods into the back of the van. The sign was yellow with black print that proclaimed, "Notice of Zone Change Request – There will be a hearing at the Monroe County Courthouse in Key West, Florida on Monday, August 19th to consider a zoning change. Request filed by L. Topper." From where I was standing I could make out the words – but just barely. There was no way in hell anybody driving by would be able too. And the whole purpose of the public announcement was supposed to be so that anybody wanting to challenge the zoning change could go to the courthouse and do so. But where these guys were planting the thing, behind the bridge abutment, it would be well-hidden.

I'd seen enough. Smelling the stench of trouble in the sultry tropical air, I cranked up the van and drove over the bridge to the Wrecker's Key side.

Back at the trailer I almost cut my thumb as I hurriedly filleted my catch. I wanted to get back over to Pa Bell's place to tell him what I'd seen. I'd have gone directly there after fishing, but I didn't knowing how long I might be there and didn't want the fish to go bad. After cleaning the last fish, my wet hands up in front of me, I stepped over to the front window and looked out across the channel. It was too far away to see the sign they'd planted on Flagler's Key, but I could well see that clump of mangroves growing out of the water along the shoreline. Of course that truck and car were long gone by then. Returning to the sink, I rinsed the fish well, placed them in a bowl, covered it with tinfoil and put it into the refrigerator. With that done, I left to go to Pa's.

After stepping outside I dropped a bag full of snapper skeletons and entrails into a plastic trash standing next to the entrance. Then I walked around to the other side of the trailer and glanced over at Julie's place.

Damn! She would be out on the porch right now. This is going to be awkward as hell ... living here with her right next door.

Dressed in short cutoff jeans and a white tee, Julie was on her toes watering one of her many hanging plants. As I stepped over to the van, I couldn't help but to watch. With her back to me, she stretched way up high – flexing her luscious calves and all-female thighs. Then she reached a little higher yet. The back of her shirt lifted out of her shorts, exposing her narrow lower back. At the bottom of her shorts, a peek of her two bare cheeks suddenly made an appearance as well. *Whoosh*, I thought, shaking my head. But I didn't want her to catch me gawking at her – for the second time that day. Forcing my eyes away, I climbed into the van.

When I closed the door she turned my way, and I leaned toward the windshield, giving her a weak little wave. She did the same thing then immediately turned right back around to her plants. As much as my gesture had been an acknowledgment of her presence, it was also an apologetic gesture. I rolled out of that driveway feeling like hell – even slimier than the fish I'd just cleaned.

Chapter 8

Pa wasn't home when I went to his place so I stopped into Barnacle Bell's later that afternoon. When I plopped down on a torn, red upholstered stool, there were only a handful of customers at the bar. It was quiet and with the front door wedged open it was a bit lighter inside than usual. Pa was breaking open rolls of coins and putting them in his old cash register. Without looking up, he asked, "What can I get ya Sonny?"

"Can of Miller Lite would work."

He set a cold, damp can on a bar coaster and said, "Saw you out on the bridge before. Any Luck?"

"I got a few snapper before the tide ran out. I also jumped a good-sized tarpon on a heavier outfit. Man, was he something."

"Yep," Pa said, "with that new moon the tides are at their lowest now. Anyway, if you got some snapper you musta found that rock pile at the edge of the channel."

"Sure did. A guy up in Big Pine at 'Big Time Bait and Tackle' told me about it."

"Cap Forest?"

"No. A friend of Forest's. A guy named Dalton Judge."

"Don't believe I know him."

After taking a swallow of beer, I said, "I did meet Captain Forest though, and he gave me a job at the shop. I'm starting tomorrow. He told me to say hello to you."

"Yep, I know him and his daddy, Franklin Munro, for a lotta years."

"Oh, I thought Forest was Caps last name."

"Nope," Pa said before taking a pull on his Lucky Strike and spraying the smoke up toward a rotating paddle fan. "Ran some Hoover's gold back in the thirties with Franklin. We was just teenagers then, but we knew our way through them mangroves like nobody else. Authorities took after us a few times, but they never had a chance of catchin' us."

"Forest seems like an okay guy," I said, "just a bit quiet."

"Yup, both him and his father are stand-up guys. Forest had some of the bootleg in his blood too. Ran some 'square grouper' a few times. That is until he got caught one day near off Lois Key – the island where the monkeys live. But that was back in the early 80's, before the law started flying over this part of the Keys in Fat Albert ... the blimp. Day Forest got caught the coasties were swarming ’round him like sand flies before he knew what hit ’im. Impounded his boat, ‘The Low Key’.”

“I guess he did time?”

“Four years at Raiford. He came out a much more serious man than when he went in. Been hittin’ the whiskey real hard ever since.”

Pa pushed back a wisp of his thin white hair then scratched the back of his head a couple of times. Figuring it was as good a time as any to tell him what I’d seen that morning I said, “I wanted to tell you something Mister Bell. Something I saw when I was fishing this morning.”

“What’s that?”

“Well, when I was leaving – walking off the bridge, a county truck and a black Mercedes pulled off the road at the foot of the bridge. This was over on the Flagler’s Key side. Anyway, two county workers planted a change-of-zoning sign behind an abutment. It seems like they were hiding it so nobody driving by would know it’s there. The suit driving the black Benz was supervising them.”

“Damn!” Pa said, suddenly narrowing his eyes real tight. “What did he look like – the guy with the suit?”

“Tall, trim, deep tan, good head of silver hair,

sharp dresser, probably in his early fifties."

"That god damned Topper!" Pa blurted, spinning his head, glancing out the front window at the road.

I then shifted my eyes that way. Heat waves undulated atop the torrid asphalt. The afternoon sun was ruthlessly hot, but not as hot as Pa had become.

"That's state land over there on Flagler's Key!" he said, balling his fists at his sides. "How the hell is he gettin' ahold of it?"

"I guess you know him," I said.

"Damned right I know him! That's Lionel Topper, some sleazy real estate baron from Michigan, came down here 'bout six years ago after tearin' up half the Midwest. He's the one responsible for most of the building goin' on in the lower keys. I knew it was just a question of time before he'd work his way up here."

Pa then snatched my empty can from the bar, crushed it tightly, and put a fresh one in front of me.

"They say that when he was up north he and his banker buddies tried to run a monastery full of monks off their property, in a place called Grassy Pointe, Michigan. They wanted to build a damn *country club* on the site. Only reason they didn't get away with that one was because the monks had been there for close to a hundred years. They had no mortgage or encumbrances."

“Yeah, I know *his type*,” I said, nodding my head. “They’ve got their own ways of getting whatever they want done. It’s their country and their laws, and if they don’t have the necessary legal tools their buddies just whip them up. Whenever they want to they either change or make laws to fit their needs.”

“Yeah. That’s exactly how it works,” Pa said, glancing now at the few other patrons at the bar. “I’ve gotta take care of them fellas. Be right back.”

As he padded down the other side of the bar I turned to the open door and squinted. Jackie Beers was rolling in on his wheelchair with Fred Sampson behind him.

“Let the games begin!” Beers howled.

Two men, commercial fisherman who obviously knew Jackie, shook their heads, shared a chuckle then resumed their conversation.

“Hey, what’s happening?” Jackie asked, as he pulled out the stool next to me with one hand and parked there – literally.

Once he’d rolled in, Fred said, “Hello,” and sat on the next stool down.

“I was just telling Mister Bell that I saw some guys put a sign, a zoning change notice, on the shore just over the bridge this morning.

"What side?" Fred asked and then held his lower lip between his teeth.

"The Gulf side. Right by the channel."

"Son of a bitch," Fred said.

"Let's get drunk and trash the County Courthouse," Jackie said. "I'm not afraid of those bastards!"

Pa had overheard us and as he placed matching boilermakers in front of Jackie and Fred, he said, "We can't go gettin crazy now. We've gotta take our time and think this thing out."

"When's this meeting, hearing, whatever they call it?" Fred asked, pensively rotating the full shot glass in front of him. Without waiting for an answer he then swallowed the drink, took a gulp of beer and said, "Sneaky bastards! What about that law they passed a few years ago that states you can't destroy coastal mangroves. They're supposed to be protected. What happened to that?"

"I'll tell you how that one works," Pa said with a hint of helplessness now in the tone of his voice. "What they did down in Cudjoe and Sugarloaf Keys was buy up a bunch a waterfront property for a song, wherever there were a lot of mangroves. Folks who owned them were told they couldn't build on 'em because the trees were protected."

"Right," Fred said, stretching out the "i" in the word as he slowly raised his head and eyebrows, "because you can't develop it. Then, after that bottom feeder Lionel Topper collected all the available lots, he built on them anyway."

"Yup," Pa said, "he bought 'em dirt cheap. Then he came in with a John Deere Payloader and mowed down all the mangroves. After that, he throws up a dock so prospective buyers would have a place to tie up their boats. This raises the value of the property even more. He even dredged channels up to those docks illegally."

"Didn't anyone report him for destroying the mangroves?" I asked.

"All of the owners lived out of the state." Pa came back. "Topper made damn sure of that. Most of 'em never even saw what was happening after they sold."

"All you have to do to find out who owns what parcel is check the tax rolls at the county courthouse down in Key West," Fred said. "Just go into the computers. They'll tell you when they took possession, their home address, and how long ago they purchased it."

Pa popped open a can of Busch for himself, took a swallow before lowering it to the bar then said, "Finally, one guy who got swindled came to Key West on business and took a drive up to see his old lot, the place he'd dreamed of retiring on. What does he see but a brand new house on it, and what a home. Damn thing looked like a castle on stilts – with not a *single* mangrove on the shoreline. They'd been cleared."

"What'd he do about it?" Sonny asked.

"He went on down to the court house screamin' and a yellin' and finally the County Commissioners agreed to take a look at the situation. Well, the guy who got ripped off went back north when his business was finished down here. The commissioners didn't address the problem till he was long gone and then they only did it because the scam had stirred some of the locals up real good. You know, the ones that care about what's left of the environment."

"Yeah, I remember that now," Jackie said. "It finally went to court and Topper's good buddy, 'The *Honorable* J.T. Simonton' heard the case. He just slapped Topper on the wrist, and gently at that."

"That's right," Pa said, as he set us all up with drinks again.

"I got this round," Jackie told Pa as he tossed a twenty on the bar. Pa left it there for the time being and then went on. "Bottom line was Topper just had to pay a fifteen-hundred-dollar fine and then only for the lot that the one guy complained about. There was no further action taken on the dozens of others he'd cleared."

"Yupper," I said, "the grand-and-a-half he had to pay was just a little overhead, an operating expense."

Still looking at me, Pa then managed a small smile and said, "You know son, I think you're gonna fit in just fine here." Then he paused for a second and held up a thick index finger. He shook it a few times as he said in a kind, good-natured tone, "Just don't be callin' me Mister Bell anymore. Okay? Call me Pa."

I stayed for one more beer and listened as the guys continued to discuss what action they might take at the August 19th hearing. There weren't many options. The best they could come up with was to march into the meeting and put up as much resistance as possible. They all knew the prognosis for Flagler's Key was not favorable. They also knew they'd be listened to in Key West, but not heard. The businessmen would get to the courthouse early, with their entourage of friends, and take up most of the seats. The handful of folks from Wrecker's Key would be made to look like nothing more than a handful of disgruntled misfits.

As I sat at the bar with these men I couldn't help but feel myself bonding to them and to their cause. Pa and Jackie may not have been overly educated men but, like Fred Sampson, they were very insightful and had a strong sense of integrity. They weren't about to let wrong trample all over right, not without putting up some kind of a fight anyway. But as much as I'd taken a liking to them and to Wrecker's Key, I had no plans on getting involved with their efforts to prevent Flagler's Key from being developed. Sure, I was all for their cause, but I already had more than enough on my plate. And as the conversation wore on, my mind eventually went off on its own – stopping at a helping on my plate that I knew all too well was going to take a long, long time to digest.

Crystal clear images of Wendy's face again started rolling through my mind. And as I studied each one closely, they were all shrouded with dark doubts. I doubted I would ever truly fit in on the small island or, for that matter, anywhere else. Sitting there on that barstool, thinking about my estranged wife, the home we had, and the life we'd once shared hurt me deeply. And as if that wasn't enough, I seriously began to doubt that I would ever be capable of loving again. After the way Wendy had betrayed me, how could I? How was I ever going to trust another woman again, let alone love her? Ever since our breakup, my past, present, and future problems had churned over and over again in my mind – abrading my spirit like so many grains of sand in a roiling surf. Oh sure, there had been other times since my previous birthday that I'd been at ease. Times like the first hour I'd spent in Barnacle Bell's that afternoon and the day before, when I'd walked through Ernest Hemingway's house. But those moments of contentment were always short-lived. They never lasted. For the most part, ever since that first moment when I realized my wife had been unfaithful, I had steadily felt my mind eating away at itself. There was no way I could stop it.

Chapter 9

As the magenta Florida sun rose from the far edge of the Atlantic the next morning, I prepared to go jogging. And the very first thought I had when I stepped outside was how fortunate I was that Julie's place was on the other side of my trailer. She very well could be out on her porch, drinking coffee. With what had taken place between us, and with everything else I had on my mind, the last thing I wanted to do so early in the morning was to make small talk. Loping along slowly at first, I headed in the opposite direction.

Just a few trailers down, I waved hello to an elderly couple who'd been tending their small garden. I didn't know them from Adam, but they waved back to me and smiled. Being the new kid on the block so to speak, I was certain they'd already heard all about me. At the time I didn't know their names were Ethel and Mordecai Cromarty nor that they were from Golden, Colorado, and had been married fifty-nine years. Short as they both were, when I passed by I couldn't help thinking how they looked like two happy little leprechauns.

Two trailers up from the Cromarty's place the Moon family was also outside. Horatio Moon was a quiet, fragile man, with shoulder-length, gun-metal hair. His wife, Eunice, put me in mind of the female half of the duet who'd sung at Barnacle Bell's two nights earlier. Eunice also parted her long hair in the middle, but she was very fond of ankle-length, paisley skirts and dresses. To see the Moons was like flashing back to 1969 Woodstock, whether you were old enough to be there or not. They lived with their six-year-old son, Joshua, in an aging, one-bedroom travel trailer with rainbow murals painted in a vivid spectrum of colors of each side of it. My hunch would later be substantiated when Pa tells me that Horatio had done the artwork himself. When I passed, the amiable couple also waved at me just before climbing into their old van.

I soon picked up my pace, jogged up the sandy road, made a left onto the narrow highway, and crossed over the Wrecker's Key Bridge. When I got to the other side I glanced back at that yellow sign down by the water then went about another mile before pushing the whole way back to the trailer. Once there, I was just about to grab the doorknob and go inside when I heard a voice. It was Sissy's. She was on the porch next door talking to Julie. I had left the small air conditioner running in my bedroom when I'd left, and low as they were speaking they surely must have thought I couldn't hear them. Not with the steady hum of the AC between my bedroom and Julie's porch. But they were wrong. I couldn't quite make out what Sissy was saying, but I did hear her say my name. Then, like the lowest form of eavesdropper I was being, I slowly stepped around to the front of my trailer. Once there, I froze with my back to the aluminum structure like a deer in a headlight.

"What a creep he turned out to be," I heard Sissy say. "And to think I thought he seemed like a nice guy!"

Then, with absolutely no malice in her tone, Julie said, "Don't jump to conclusions and pass judgment so quickly, Sissy. Like I said before, you don't know what happened. And, really, it wasn't anything major."

"I know you Julie, and I know somethin's botherin' you. Plus, I *know* he spent the night here. I saw him leaving yesterday mornin', when I was goin' to open up the store."

"Certain things are personal, Sissy, and private things should remain that way. I'm not going to talk about it. But I will tell you this – it means an awful lot to me that you're so concerned."

There was a short pause at that point in the conversation. Still motionless, with the hot sun beating down me I figured they were looking at each other. Then Julie broke the silence saying, "And don't worry. Everything will be fine."

"Well, I still don't like him anymore."

"Don't say that. I know that deep inside he's a decent and sensitive person. He's just got things troubling him right now."

"A lot of us had problems when we came down here," Sissy came back. "I never told you this, but the day I left Indiana two years ago I was in my nightgown, bendin' over, scopin' out the refrigerator to see what I could get for breakfast. Well anyway, when I reached inside for the milk is when it happened. My father came up behind me and leaned up against my ass ... "

"Oh my God, Sissy! No!"

"Yeah he did. He grabbed a hold of my breasts too."

"What the hell did you do?"

"I let out a long, loud scream, turned around, and gave him an elbow, hard as I could right in the face. He let go then ... put his hand to his nose then saw blood all over his fingers. I was still a screamin' and started to run for my room. My ma still was still in bed with one of her hangovers but when she heard all the hollerin' she got up and came down the stairs. I didn't make it that far. My sonofabitchin' father dove and tackled me before I could even make it out of the kitchen. Well ... I went down hard, face first on the floor. Put a dimple in the linoleum when I broke my tooth."

"That bastard!"

“He sure is, but that wasn’t the end of it, Julie. Before I could get up he was on top a me – poundin’ away with both his fists. ’Bout that time my mother finally comes into the room. What do you think she says?”

“I don’t know. What?”

“She says, ‘What’s she done this time?’ Then my old man lies, ‘She told me to fuck myself when I said good mornin’ to ’er.’ He then gave me a couple more body shots, but he was all winded. They didn’t hurt all that much.”

“I am so, so sorry, Sissy. You told everybody here that you had to leave an abusive home, but I had no idea ....”

“Yeah, I know. I just never wanted to talk about it. Anyhow, once I broke away from his grip I ran up to my room, locked the door, jimmied a chair beneath the knob, dressed real quick like then climbed out the window with two pillowcases fulla clothes. I don’t think they called the cops or anything. They were probably afraid they’d get in trouble. Anyways, I beat heels down the road, hitchhiked to I-65 and headed straight to Florida. I coulda gone anywhere. But I wanted to be where it was warm.”

“That was awfully dangerous, Sissy – hitchhiking all the way down here.”

“Not as dangerous as stayin’ there was. Anyway, four days later, I rode into Key West in the back of a truck. I musta been somethin’ ta see – sitting up there real high on top of a load of watermelons.”

After a brief pause in their conversation, Sissy changed the subject by saying, “Come on Julie, you’ve gotta stay away from him.”

“Oh ... I think I will be staying away from him. I’m afraid I won’t be having any choice.”

“Whaddaya mean?”

“Let’s just say the reason he left so abruptly this morning was ... well, a physical thing.”

“Wait a minute! Do you mean he split because of your ....”

“Yes, my hand, Sissy. He left because of my ... my missing fingers.”

“So that’s why he’s avoiding you! What the hell makes him think he’s so perfect? You’re the most beautiful woman I’ve ever seen. *You’re* too damn good for *him*.”

“Sometimes things aren’t exactly as they seem, Sissy. Let’s just relax and take things as they come.”

Sissy then said, “I’ve gotta go. Gotta open the store in ten minutes. I’ll stop back over this afternoon."

Quickly, I tiptoed back around the trailer and ducked inside – gently closing the door behind me. I was disgusted with myself. I knew better than ever that Julie was a very special person. And I was still deeply attracted to her. Despite what I had thought up to that point, I was now beginning to believe there just might be one more woman in the world who I could trust. For the rest of the morning and all that afternoon, I wrestled with that possibility. I also kept questioning whether or not I could ever accept Julie's two flaws. Emotionally sapped by the time I went to bed, I was still grappling with myself. I turned and tossed and must have flipped that pillow over a dozen times before finally falling off to sleep. Even then I wasn't at peace.

I dreamed it was my previous birthday again. Everything seemed so real. I had driven home through the snow after quitting my job, but there was no black Lexus parked in front of my house. When I went inside, Wendy was still in bed, fast asleep. I woke her and told her what had happened at Searcy's. Seeing the concern tightening up my face she sat up in bed, patted the mattress, and said, "Sit down, Sonny." I did. And she put her arms around my head. Pulling it next to hers – cheek to cheek, she whispered in my ear, "Don't worry, honey. We'll get through this. We always do." She then reached beneath her pillow and pulled out two airline tickets to a tropical island. A short time later, after packing, we backed the van out of the driveway and headed slowly through the slush toward Kennedy Airport. We were only two houses past our place when I looked in the rearview mirror. Only then did Steve Silverman's Lexus pulling up in front our house. I could see his face behind his windshield. He looked angry as all hell. I said nothing to Wendy. I just smiled.

Chapter 10

The days flashed by and before I realized it I'd been living in the Keys for almost a full month. The job at Big Time Bait and Tackle was going well and, as cheaply as I was living, I only had to dip into the money I'd come to Florida with a couple of times. Once time I had to buy extra gas for a trip up to Key Largo, the other time when I'd bought a set of secondhand weights at a flea market in Big Pine. It felt good to be working out once again. Three days a week I lifted alongside the trailer – and not the side facing Julie's porch.

I only saw Julie a handful of times, always when she was coming or going in her VW. I well knew that she, too, was intentionally keeping plenty of distance between us. The few times we had seen each other we always put on the same forced smiles, gave a wave then went back about our business. Nevertheless, every time I saw that woman she still looked more stunning than the last. But isn't that how it always works? When you're deeply attracted to someone that you know you can't have it always seems to add to their allure. Often I thought about our affair, and how I reacted to what I'd seen that morning. I still felt terrible about it, but I didn't know what to do.

On one particular day I'd gotten a late start and had to work out in the afternoon. Never again would I do that. It was god-awful hot. By the time I finished I was all pumped-up alright, but sweating like a broiled chicken. I couldn't wait to get back inside to the air conditioning but first I wanted to take a peek at myself in the side window of my van. After stacking the weights neatly and sliding them under the trailer, I walked around and took a quick glance at my reflection in the dark glass. Reasonably satisfied with what I saw, I was just about to turn around when I noticed Julie's blue bug coming up the road. I couldn't very well high-tail it back inside the trailer. Julie would know for sure what I was doing. Instead I just fooled with the luggage rack on top of the van until she pulled in next to her place.

I stepped around the back of the van and said, "Hi." as she got out. Again she gave me the standard wave, with her right hand, and said, "Hello, Sonny. How are you?"

"I'm okay. Hot out isn't it."

"Sure is," Julie came back. Then she turned and opened up the car's trunk. I could see it was full of grocery bags. As she reached in and started grabbing at the plastic bags I approached her tentatively.

"Can I give you a hand?" I asked, unsure of what kind of response the friendly gesture would generate, hoping she wouldn't just tell me to get lost.

"No thanks. I think I'm fine," her voice came from

inside the trunk. Standing alongside her by then I noticed her carefully curl the fingers of her left hand underneath one of the bags before straightening back up. Once she did, she tossed her head back in an unsuccessfully attempt to whisk away a long lock of raven hair that had fallen over her eyes. Small droplets of perspiration had risen from her forehead, and I thought she looked a bit jittery, maybe even perturbed.

"Please, Julie, I'd really like to help," I said in a low, sincere voice.

She didn't answer me right away. Instead she looked at my face and searched it – as if looking for clues. Then her eyes rested on mine, and I detected a hint of wariness when she said, "Well ... sure, if you want to."

I hoisted the rest of the bags from the trunk, closed it then stepped ahead quickly to open the porch door for her. This wasn't the first time I'd felt clumsy around Julie.

Over the previous few weeks I'd of course been thinking about Wendy a lot. But I'd just recently admitted to myself that what we had for so long was finally over. I knew I'd always have sentimental memories, that I'd take them to my grave. I also knew that, for the rest of my life, I'd continue to hurt from time to time. I had loved Wendy and loved her hard, but I *could* feel myself healing a little more each day. I knew my pain would never go away completely –

that there would always be a void in my heart and inside my soul. But the worst of it was now behind me.

After Julie unlocked the trailer door, I followed her inside. Her window-mounted air conditioner was laboriously humming and a welcome burst of arctic-like air greeted us both.

"You can put them over there, on the table," Julie said, "How about a cold drink ... maybe a Gatorade?"

"Sure. That would really hit the spot"

"Let me just put these refrigerated things away. You might want to wait on the porch," she said, turning away to put a small chicken in the freezer. "Perspiring the way you are you'll catch a death of a cold in here. You get a Florida cold it'll take forever to shake."

During the long relentless throes of a tropical summer, the sun scorches, the air is dense and humid, and even the rain comes down hot. But when I went out on the porch like I was told to, it was actually comfortable out there. Sitting in the shade with a gentle new breeze coming in off the Gulfstream, I was just fine. Well, not really *fine*. I was nervous as hell again. Having a few moments to think about where a conversation with Julie might go certainly didn't help. Would she bring up what had happened between us?

Would I have to wiggle and make up lame excuses like I did the morning I left her alone in her bed? Suddenly I felt like kicking myself. I shouldn't have agreed to come in and have a drink with her.

With Julie taking what seemed like an extra-long time inside, and me trying not to think about what was to come, I looked around at the panoramic view before me. Way off to the left, where the Gulf of Mexico met the sky, an enormous dark thunderhead looked as though it was boiling on the horizon. Gunmetal gray in color, laced pink by the late afternoon sun, I could hear the swelling cloud rumble in the distance. Not close enough to be of any concern, I then turned my attention across the aqua channel. A bumpy green line of mangrove trees bordered the entire shoreline of Flagler's Key. Beyond them the island was dense with tall palms, some of their long spindly trunks bent in different directions. As I rolled my eyes along the wide stretch of land, I imagined it to be much like the place where Robinson Crusoe had been marooned. But when the Wrecker's Key Bridge came into view my eyes stopped moving. Again, I tried to focus on the area where that yellow sign was planted.

"Here you are," Julie then said, stepping out of trailer with the two glasses of Gatorade.

I thanked her, took a long swallow then nodded at the bridge to our right. "Have you heard they want to build something over there on Flagler Key?"

"Yes I have – resort, everybody's upset about it."

"A resort! Of all the things they can ruin that island with that's got to be the worst. If they get away with that, things are going to be a lot different around here."

"Yes they will," Julie said in a mournful tone, her eyes taking on a vacant look like someone who was about to lose something very dear to them. "Everybody here is devastated. And poor Pa ... I've never seen him act so withdrawn. I don't know what's going on in his mind – what he might do, but it scares me. He especially doesn't deserve this. He's the kindest man I've ever known."

"Yeah, he sure seems like a super guy," I said. "He told me the other day that the entire key was state-owned land. Any word about how that character Lionel Topper got ahold of it?"

"Yes. We did some checking. It seems he and Monroe County struck up a sweetheart deal with their connections in Tallahassee."

"What kind of a deal?" I asked, feeling my eyes narrow and the skin on my forehead folding up.

"It's very simple. The county buys the land from the state, and then the commissioners sell it to Topper for a so-called 'nominal fee'."

"Those snakes!"

"The icing on the cake is that the *nominal fee* is just a fraction of what the property is really worth."

"Terrific. The old 'your tax dollars at work' spiel once again," I said, looking as though I'd just swallowed a wedge of lemon that had gone bad.

"That's exactly right. They buy the property with tax dollars so that Topper can build a five-star resort. He gets richer – the politicians get their usual kickbacks – they all claim that the place will bring more jobs to the county. That's their old standby excuse, the same sorry excuse politicians at all levels use time and time again. Do you have any idea how much those jobs pay, Sonny?"

"I can only imagine! Do you know if the county purchased the land yet?"

"No, they haven't. They're holding off until the rezoning is officially approved. They already have a written commitment from the state. Once it's rezoned at the courthouse all they'll have to do is cut the state a check and set up a rush-rush, hush-hush closing with Topper."

"What's the land zoned for now?" I asked.

"Would you believe a nature preserve!

"Yeah," I said, shaking my head as I looked out beyond the channel again. "I can believe it alright. So, in essence, what's going to happen is the county's going to buy land that *already* belongs to the state's taxpayers – using the *county* taxpayers' money. Talk about pathetic."

"Yes, that's exactly what they want to do."

There was a pause then. Our conversation, despite the disheartening subject, was going far smoother than I had expected. And I could tell Julie felt the same way. She now looked at me for a moment, and I mean *looked* at me. Just like she had before what happened in her bedroom that morning, I could see the same special fondness in her eyes as she studied my face.

Finally, she broke the silence saying, "Your perception is truly uncanny, Sonny Raines."

"Don't you see it that way?" I asked.

"Oh yes, exactly that way."

She smiled then, exposing two rows of gleaming-white teeth and went on. "It's just that ... well, I think you have an exceptional ability to look at a situation, analyze it and then put it so perfectly into words."

"Really? All I've ever done is told things as I see them."

"Anyway, we're getting off the subject here," Julie went on, "Do you remember me telling you that I work part-time in Key West?"

"Yes. I sure do."

"Well, I waitress down there three days a week – at an upscale restaurant called The Golden Conch House. Usually I work afternoons, but last night I had to go in and cover for a friend of mine. She's a hostess there and needed the night off. Anyway, I was standing at the greeting station when Lionel Topper and some of his confidantes came in. There were quite a few of them, and the only table large enough to accommodate them was right behind the station. After I sat them down, I went back to my stand and listened very closely to parts of their conversation."

"Don't tell me. They were talking about Flagler's Key."

"That's right. Counting Topper there were six of them there – an even half-dozen of Monroe County's most successful bottom feeders. Carlton Webb was there. He's Key West's most successful real estate attorney and, ever-so-conveniently, State Senator Roland Webb's twin brother. Campbell Bryant was there too. A third generation builder, his family is second only to Henry Flagler himself when it comes to developing the Florida Keys."

Julie paused then. She picked up her glass of Gatorade – with her right hand of course, took a sip of the orange drink then continued. "The fourth man I recognized was a little bald guy that looks like Mister Magoo with glasses. Always with an expensive Cuban cigar in hand, Oscar Giddleman is the accountant for everyone who is anyone in KW. Anyway, it didn't take them long to get half-pickled. I was standing with my back to them, and had to leave a few times to seat customers, but I still got an earful."

"Boy," I said, "do they sound like a cast of bad actors."

"They sure are! It's true what they say about birds of a feather."

"What did they say?"

"Well, it didn't take them very long to get half-pickled on martinis and whatever else they were drinking last night. I think they were talking louder than they realized. Anyway, Carlton Webb the lawyer said he didn't see them hitting any snags in the deal, as long as they move quickly. He said as long as they did “the damn environmentalists” wouldn’t have enough time to build up any momentum. Bryant, the builder, assured Topper that their buddy the judge down there would only slap him on the wrist after he tears down the mangroves. Bryant said the judge was obligated to hand out the usual token fine so it would keep what he called the “Sierra types” quiet. He also said that Topper should get four or five crews going at the same time. That way Topper could level the two miles of shoreline he wants to in no time. Bryant also told him he should do it at night.”

Shaking my head in disbelief now, I said, “Talk about the lowest of the low.”

“They sure are. They want to excavate at night when there will be virtually no resistance. And Giddleman said he’d arrange it with the sheriff so that there’d be no patrol cars within miles of Flagler’s the night they do the job.”

“Shit, this just gets uglier and uglier. Did they say when they were planning to do it?”

“No,” Julie said, shaking her own head then in a defeated way, “if they did, it was when I had to leave to seat customers. But I did hear Bryant say something about the possibility of getting some resistance from, and I quote, ‘the bunch of misfits living in a dilapidated old trailer park across the channel from Flagler’s Key.’ He also mentioned he’d had trouble before with old Man Bell – the owner of that *garbage collection of tin cans*. Can you imagine?

"Yeah, I can. There are all kinds of people out there. Believe me ... I've met more than my share."

I then reached to a front pocket of my denim shorts but quickly realized I'd left my cigarettes in the trailer when I'd gone outside to lift weights. That was when Julie told me the very worst of the news. Her face took on a look of deep, deep concern when she said, "The last thing I heard before they all left to go to a place called Hugs and Jugs is what bothers me the most. I mean it *really* frightens me."

"Tell me. What's bothering you?" I did not like seeing her looking so fearful.

She breathed in deeply, let it out then said, "Well ... Giddleman gave Topper a phone number. He told him to make the call at a payphone outside the strip joint as soon as they got there. The number is Brock Blackburn's. Sonny, he's Key West's most dangerous character. Everybody knows who he is. He just recently got out of Raiford – the state prison! It was the third time he'd been up there. Once before he did time for manslaughter, and everyone knows that the man he killed wasn't the first. Just thinking of this guy sends chills up my spine."

"What are you saying, Julie? You think Topper's going to contract this lunatic to hit somebody?"

“I think he wants to have Blackburn at the ready. In case he needs him.”

“Oh shit, this is not good,” I said, bringing a hand up to my chin. “You think he might turn him loose on Pa, don’t you?”

“He very well could. Pa is *not* going to take this sitting down. And anybody else who gets in the way would be in jeopardy as well. Oh God ... I don’t like any of this. Why did this have to happen?”

Julie was fighting back tears by now. Again it bothered the hell out of me. And I of course didn’t like seeing Pa in danger either. But my hands were tied. What could I do? I hadn’t come to the Keys to get involved in anything like this.

“Look, Julie,” I said reaching across the table between us, resting my hand on her bouncing shoulder, looking into her reddening eyes. “Stay strong. You don’t know for sure that anything is going to come of this. Things sometimes have a way of looking far worse than they really are.” That’s what I said alright, but it wasn’t much consolation to either of us. Julie well knew that I was only trying to downplay the situation. She knew it as well as I did.

She sniffled then and her eyes turned to the road. “Here comes Sissy. It’s time for her lesson. I’ve been helping her prepare for her G.E.D. She wants to get it and start taking classes at Florida Keys Community

College, on Stock Island. I've got to pull myself together here. Please, don't mention any of what I told you to her."

"Of course not, I've got to get going anyway. I don't want to hold you girls up, and I need to get cleaned up," I said rising to my feet. I certainly didn't feel like dealing with Sissy at this point, particularly with all the new negative clutter churning wildly inside my head. "I'll talk to you soon, Julie, okay?"

She also stood up then, and she glanced at my bare chest. It made me felt a little self-conscious, but I liked it as well. She looked absolutely incredible. You just don't see women like her every day, not even in the biggest of cities.

"Sonny," she said, "if you get up early tomorrow how about stopping over for coffee?"

Feeling the corners of my mouth rise into a small, heartfelt smile then, I said, "I'd like that, but I don't know for sure if I can. Buster called me at the tackle shop yesterday and asked if I wanted to go tarpon fishing with him and the guys tonight. I don't know how late we'll be out. But if I wake up enough, and you're out here that early, sure, I'll stop over before going to work."

"Either way, be careful tonight, you hear? Stay on the alert. Topper and that crowd can play awfully rough. Is Pa going with you?"

"I think so."

"Watch out for him too, please. Those lunatics might not wait to be provoked"

I was going to tell her not to be silly – not to overreact at this point, but I didn't. The last thing she'd said had me thinking in directions I didn't want to go. Nevertheless, I said, "Sure, Julie. I'll keep an eye out."

Then I left.

Chapter 11

At the tackle shop the minutes and hours dragged by like you wouldn't believe. When I checked my watch countless times, I could have sworn the thing was moving backwards. Then, of all the days to be late, Cap's wife Maggie didn't relieve me until a quarter after five! Not wanting to miss the fishing trip for the world, I bee-lined it back to Wrecker's the moment she came in the door; left the van at the trailer, and double-timed it straight to Pa's dock.

By the time I arrived all the guys were already onboard the cabin cruiser. Pa, Fred, and Jackie, all with a beer can in hand, were watching Buster expertly throw a nine-foot cast net from the stern. I could see it as I walked out on the dock. Sailing wide open, in a perfect circle, the nylon mesh encompassed a small school of mullet school when it hit the water. The boat captain let it sink a few seconds then started hauling the long rope in, hand over hand. That's when Jackie Beers spotted me. In his usual hoarse voice he shouted out good-naturedly, "Get your ass into this tub, we wanna catch the tide!" He then took a gulp from what was probably his umpteenth Budweiser of the day.

As I climbed over the boat's gunwale, Buster pulled the net out of the water and opened it over a live well. About a dozen mullet splashed into the bait well, but two of the pungent smelling fish fell to the deck and started flopping around. Quickly, I scooped them up and flipped them in with their school mates. Grabbing a rag, I then glanced at the four well-maintained fishing outfits protruding straight up out of the boat's rod holders and asked Buster if I should have brought my own tackle?

Carefully lowering the now empty net, weights first into a five-gallon bucket, he said, "Nope. Got everything we need."

Pa, who was standing at the helm, then turned on the ignition. As if objecting at first the twin inboards rumbled a bit but in no time at all smoothed into a steady assuring hum.

"Grab a beer," Fred said, pointing to an Igloo cooler way back in the stern.

I popped one open, took a swallow, lit a smoke, and savored a familiar feeling of excitement as the powerful engines labored beneath my feet.

It was a windless evening, the air thick and humid. The southern sun was creeping toward the western horizon, and as far as I could see in that direction the calm water and wide sky were both turning a surreal pink. To the north, near Marathon, there was a small gathering of thunderheads. But they were a good ways off.

A few minutes later *The Island Belle* slowly made its way up the channel toward the Wreckers Key Bridge. Carefree and jovial, all the men were horsing around by giving each other a ribbing. But as we closed in on the bridge's tall pilings, all of that came to an abrupt stop. I could *feel* everybody's high spirits taking a sudden nosedive. There was a long row of newly-planted survey stakes running along Flagler's Key shoreline. For five minutes not a word was uttered. I may have been a newbie, and didn't have as strong a tie to the island as the other guys, but I too felt a profound sense of loss. During the silence I tried to imagine how the Bell's must have felt and what they might be thinking. The ambiance was funereal – as if the four good buddies were gathered around the grave of a recently departed fifth friend.

It wasn't until after we had motored under the bridge, and those wooden stakes were out of sight, that Jackie Beers finally broke the silence. Sitting in his wheelchair, inside the cockpit next to Pa who was at the wheel, he tried to elevate the mood by saying in a good-natured tone, "Okay, Sonny boy, we all kicked in for gas and I covered your end. How about forkin' over a ten spot?" I stepped over to them, pulled out my wallet, and handed Jackie a ten. As I stuffed the billfold back in my pocket, I glanced at Pa Bell. Staring through the windshield as if he detested what he saw on the other side of the glass, he turned the boat north then slammed the throttle lever all the way forward. The boat lurched hard, and in nothing flat the hull was up on plane – hauling along the ocean's surface. Nobody said another word during the run up to Bahia Honda Channel.

In the waning light, just before turning into Bahia Honda Channel, Pa again suddenly swung the boat hard, seaward, to avoid a surfacing loggerhead. The turtle was huge. Probably five feet in length, and its head looked like a coconut floating on the ocean's surface; a green, unripe coconut. Spooked by the boat, it submerged back into its silent world as quickly as it had appeared. With the creature out of harm's way, Pa then expertly swung *The Island Belle* back to the port side and slowly brought her down off plane. Minutes later we were idling beneath the old Bahia Honda Bridge.

As he killed the engines Pa looked to the north, but not very far. We were much closer to those storm clouds now than we were when leaving Wrecker's. And they were still drifting toward us. A cloud-to-ocean lightning bolt lit up the sky as well as all the faces in the boat. Hurriedly, Buster lowered the anchor.

"Let's get the baits in the water." he said, yanking a thumb at the grumbling thunderhead. "Maybe we can get an hour in before *she* busts loose."

"You sure it'll hit us?" I asked.

"She'll be here," Pa said, as a great blue heron

glided by us on its way to find a safe roost. “Grab a mullet and hook it through the lips,” Pa said, looking and nodding at me.

“They’ll stay alive longer in the strong current if they’re held head-first into it,” Buster added. “Allows water to enter their mouth and pass through their gills.”

Just as Jackie, Fred and I lowered our wiggling baits into the seemingly black, nighttime water, the boat began to rock a bit. In an instant the wind had picked up and the water became ruffled. I lit a cigarette and took a sip of beer. Then something startled me.

My eyes jerked down to the big reel in my left hand. The spool was revolving quickly, line ripping off faster and faster in erratic tugs. Then, about twenty yards out, the hapless mullet at the end of my line suddenly broke the surface. With the cabin lights illuminating the area around the boat, I could see the frantic fish out there trying to stay airborne for fear of what was under the water beneath it. As I watched I could also hear the doomed bait-fish’s small splashes out there as well. Then there was another splash – a loud crash really. It looked like a small bomb had exploded! Water flew in all directions as a hundred-pound-plus marine acrobat blasted the surface.

Propelled by its foot-wide tail, the tarpon immediately dove to deeper water. Gently, I thumbed the revolving spool to prevent it from backlashing. It took every ounce of discipline I could muster not to set the hook. But I knew the big fish needed time to turn the mullet headfirst in its cavernous mouth before swallowing it. Thump-thump-thump-thump-thump, I could feel my hopped-up heart caroming off the sides of its ribbed cage. Ten, twenty, thirty more yards I let it swim. Then it came time. I engaged the reel's spool, let the line yank the rod tip almost all the way down to the water then reared back. Three times in succession I jerked the rod, hard, putting my back and shoulders behind every yank. The needle-sharp hook struck home. It penetrated the powerful fish's boney jaw.

"I got him! I got him!" I hollered to the others as the silver monster catapulted from the water somewhere out in the darkness. A second later it landed back on the surface, and it sounded like a full grown man had belly-whopped from the bridge. Again water splayed everywhere – this time beyond the glow of the boat's lights. Way out there in the black, moonless night, the splash created a spectacular light-show of neon phosphorescence. Then the huge fish sounded. It dove deeper and deeper into the eerie depths of the channel. Straining now to hang onto the bouncing, bucking rod, I felt as if I had a crazed mustang tied to the business end of the line."

"Way to go!" Jackie shouted excitedly, spilling some of his beer on his pants.

"Keep the tip up," Fred coached, "just like you're

doing."

I didn't say anything, neither did Pa or Buster. Calm as could be, they both just watched me. Over the years they had seen thousands of fishermen under pressure. Now they were assessing the way I handled a rod. It was important to me that I impressed them. Real sport fishermen, like all true sportsmen, take deep pride in how well they perform when they do the one thing they are most passionate about.

The mighty fish jumped a few more times then took off like a runaway freight train again. Up to this point I'd been cranking the reel with my right hand, supporting the rod with the other. My left forearm felt like it was pumped-up to twice its normal size. Each time the tarpon had jumped it shook its massive head so hard that the rod tip jolted frantically from side to side. Nevertheless, I thought I had things pretty much under control. But then things changed. My heart stood still when I felt the fish's broad, swishing tail slapping the line as it sounded once again. Then there was nothing. The line went slack. I was sure that the tarpon frayed the monofilament line and had broken free.

"He cut me," I said, "unless he's coming in."

"He is!" Buster yelled out in a rare display of excitement. "He's comin' towards us! Reel! Reel like hell!"

Then Pa chimed in, “He’ll jump again. That’s when he’ll throw the hook – unless you get that slack out. Crank! Keep crankin’!”

With my palms and fingers wet with perspiration, it was tough to keep the reel’s handle from slipping out of my grip, but I managed. And I kept reeling like a madman. Little by little, I brought in the slack until I’d recouped most of the line. Finally I could feel the fish’s weight again. Beads of sweat streamed my forehead and cheeks, dripping off my chin. My breathing was heavy and rapid.

“He’s going to jump!” Fred Sampson bellowed above the torrential rain as it pummeled the water all around us.

“Be sure to bow the rod tip toward to him,” Buster added, “when he breaks the surface!”

Silently, we all watched the line as it lifted out of the cresting waves. The fish was rushing up from the depths. With my bent knees now leaning against the side of the boat for support, I was struggling to keep up with the fish but kept reeling and reeling. I thought all the hard work and excitement would never end. But that thought was a short-lived. What was about to happen would instantaneously clear *all* our minds.

Not ten feet from *The Island Belle’s* stern the fish erupted from the water. Up, up, up – water flying everywhere, the creature rose like an angry silver missile. Its entire body cleared the surface and it shimmied and danced atop its sweeping tail.

"Would ya look at that?" Jacky Beers shouted as his wheelchair bumped into my leg.

Right before our eyes, the huge fish suspended itself in the thick humid air. We were so close to it we could clearly hear its massive gills rattling like two loco castanets. Frantically, like a berserk bulldog, it was shaking its head from side to side. Certainly it was trying to throw the hook, but it seemed to be saying to me, "No, no, no, no! You're not going to win this battle."

It was an incredible performance. Watching this prehistoric gladiator, its glistening sides armored with silver dollar sized scales, was an event I'd never forget. I didn't have time to stop and think about it, but this was one of those amazing images I would be able to pull from my memory for the rest of my life. A picture I'd visualize with life-like clarity.

Finally the tarpon lost out to the law of gravity and it fell – headfirst in our direction. It landed so close to the boat that all of us got a warm saltwater shower. Wiping the spray from his face, Buster said, "I've seen 'em land in boats before. I know lots of guides who've had bow rails bent, and worse, from big tarpon." Those last words no sooner left his mouth when thunder boomed and the brightest network of spidery white lightning yet lit the entire sky.

“Hell of a cooker comin’, Sonny. You better get this fish in soon,” Pa said.

“Then we’ll make a run for it,” Buster added with a hint of concern in his voice. “We just might be able to beat this storm back to the dock.”

The fish was tiring. No longer was it making any desperate runs. Instead, it swam slowly in shrinking circles on the surface before us. Leaning back on the rod, I steadily led it toward me. When I got it alongside the boat the old fish tried one last trick. As if suddenly injected with adrenaline, it tried to dart under the boat. Quickly, it yanked the rod tip into the sea water below. I pulled back once again – harder than any other time during the encounter. Finally, he stopped. I’d managed to prevent the line from scraping the hull. But for a few more seconds it was still a standoff – him fighting for his freedom – me fighting just for a moment’s glory. At last, I pulled the fish out from underneath and back alongside the boat. It just laid there exhausted, on the surface, its broad tail waving slowly like a white flag after a battle.

At that exact moment the rain started to fall. Heavy drops the size of dimes started pelting me, the rest of the men, the fish, the boat and the water. As if someone in the dark heavens above had thrown a switch, a blustery cool wind howled in out of the north. Buster grabbed a gaff hook from the recessed storage area in the gunwale, turned his Redman cap backwards on his head so as not to lose it then glanced over his shoulder at the approaching storm. The tarpon was still on its side, head first in the current; its spirit not broken, but its body exhausted.

With a gloved paw, Buster reached over the side and grabbed the leader just beneath the swivel. Gently, he slid the gaff into the fish's lower jaw and lifted it partially out of the water. We all leaned over the side, assessing it in awe. It was a giant of its species by any sportsman's standards.

"I'll bet she'd go one-eighty; one-eighty-five," Buster said as the rain came down even harder.

"That's one goliath of a fish," Jackie slurred, as he gave me a light, celebratory punch in the shoulder.

Still leaning over the side and holding the line, Buster said, "Sonny, get those pliers outta my sheath and pull this hook out." The long blond hair beneath his cap now lifting wildly, he appraised the position of the fish hook.

I grabbed the pliers, and removed the five-aught hook by rocking it side to side and pushing at the same time.

"Turn around you guys," Pa then said, standing behind us with his hand protecting the lens of a Pentax. We all turned; Buster hoisted the fish high as he could, and the camera flashed – along with another bolt of lightning. Hurriedly, Pa put the camera back inside the cockpit, and Buster leaned back over the side. As he lowered the "silver king" back into the water, big waves – seemingly angry waves slammed one after another into the side of the boat. Rocking hard as we were, Buster had all he could do to hold the fish headfirst in the current.

With the rain and wind now coming at us with all the force of a tropical storm, the boat was really rocking and rolling. Pa had had enough. He turned over the engines then bellowed above them and the wind, "Come on! Let's get the hell outta here!"

"Just a damn minute," Buster barked back over his shoulder, "I need another minute!"

He was still trying to resuscitate the fish, and it was working. The flowing water of the flood tide was bringing life-sustaining oxygen into the fish's respiratory system. Side by side, in the pouring rain, the four of us watched as the beats of its tail grew stronger. Finally, when the time was right, Buster released his grip on the tarpon's lower lip. Able to keep itself upright now, it hesitated for just a moment then slowly started making its way back into the black depths of the channel. Once it was out of sight, and Buster was relieved no sharks had been lying in wait he shouted, "Okay! Kick it in gear!"

Pa didn't need to be told twice. He gunned it immediately and *The Island Belle* lurched forward. All the rest of us grabbed onto the side so as not to take a tumble and crash into the stern. As we clutched the fiberglass another nasty bolt of lightning struck nearby. Only two hundred yards away, this one lit up the swimming beach on the Bahia Honda State Park shoreline. Once Pa got the boat up on plane we all made a dash for the cockpit. It surely wasn't the safest place to be in a storm like this, but we all felt a bit more secure in there. Nobody said a word as we sped out of the channel and into the unsheltered waters of the now turbulent Atlantic.

Thrilled as I was to have caught the prize tarpon, this was no night to be cruising in a boat. Oh sure, when I was still with Wendy, back in New York, I had been in my share of rough seas. Several times, while winter fishing for cod off Montauk Point, the boat I'd been on had to head in early because of snow and rough seas. But this was different. I was far more nervous this time. The electrical storm's highly-charged winds were energizing the ocean's surface into a frothy mess. Out in the darkness, all around *The Island Belle*, legions of menacing, white-capped demons seemed to be doing some kind of angry, ritualistic dance. I'd never seen anything like it before. The waves seemed to be charging us from all directions. They were tall waves too, huge breakers and close as they were to one another, only made the situation all the more precarious. Between the waves, the rain and the ungodly wind it seemed like Mother Ocean had been possessed – like she was searching in the darkness for something to sacrifice.

Able as the cruiser was, it was barely making it over the top of each wave. And each time it cleared one, the bow pounded back onto the water so hard my teeth chattered. I could live with that, the rain, and the wind, but there was all that lightning as well. It was now cracking all around us, sometimes two bolts at once. And the thunder, it was deafening. Every time it resonated the entire boat shivered as if it were scared to death. Even with all the beer Jackie had drunk that day, I could still see plenty of fear in his eyes as he clung to the back of Buster's seat.

Buster had taken over the helm for Pa, and I could hear the tenseness in his voice when he said, "Damn! I hate lightening!"

"I don't blame you," I shouted, as the horizontal rain whipped into the cockpit. "I've never been in a T storm like this one."

"'Bout four years ago," Buster came back, "I was standin' on the dock behind the house and got knocked plumb on my ass by a strike."

"You get hurt?"

"Nah, but when it first hit I thought it was all over. I remember smelling this ... this *sulphur* like smell – like burning matches."

With the danger we were now in, the last thing I needed to hear about was Buster being hit by lightning. But I was his guest and, like everybody else onboard, I was doing the best I could to hide my anxiety.

"What was it like? What did it feel like?" I asked.

"Felt like somebody came up from behind and whacked me square on the top of the head with a lead pipe."

"Yeah," Pa then said. "I told 'im to come in off that dock."

"Hell, Pa, how many times I got to tell you? 'Cept for some nasty clouds just startin' to show on the horizon the whole sky was clear."

"Yeah, yeah, yeah!" Pa came back again. "They were dark, nasty, *ink-blue* clouds. And I told you it wasn't safe out there."

There was an uncomfortable pause in the conversation then. Obviously the father and son had been down this road before, more than once. In an attempt to lessen the tension between them, I said, "I didn't know that lightening from a storm that far away could hit somebody."

"Well it sure got me! I'm lucky as hell to still be here."

For the next ten minutes, nobody said much of anything. Nervous eyes clicked back and forth and we all flinched every time thunder boomed overhead and lightning lit up the cockpit. Laboriously, the boat ploughed ahead until, suddenly, we were out of the storm. Quick as you could snap your fingers we passed through the outer edge of the god awful, life-threatening squall. Just like that the wind let up, the rain ceased, and the sea settled into smaller, smoother waves. The storm was still following us toward Wrecker's Key, but we were finally out of it and would easily beat it back to the dock.

Right away everybody except Buster stepped out onto the deck and headed straight for the beer cooler. Pa grabbed two cans and went back into the cockpit with his son. Fred and Jackie struck up a conversation about what we'd just been through. And I looked out at the starry half of the dark Florida sky in front of us. With *The Island Belle* quickly picking up speed now, I reached into my pocket for my cigarettes. They were soaking wet, but that was okay. All that really mattered was that we were safe now. Or so I thought.

It wasn't long before Buster eased back on the throttle, and we rounded the buoy leading into Wrecker's channel. The area around the bridge was a no-wake zone so we approached it ever so slowly. The low hum of the idling engines was the only sound to be heard in the dark, Florida Keys night. That is, until we passed through the two rows of towering concrete pilings. The moment *The Island Belle* cleared the bridge and came out the other side Jackie Beers suddenly let out a scream so loud it could probably be heard all the way down the channel to the trailer park.

"OH HELL! LOOK! IT LOOKS LIKE THE STORE'S ON FIRE!"

Instantly, we all jerked our heads to the port side. The boat was still moving ever so slowly across the water, but we could only get one quick glimpse down the Overseas Highway before the road and store would be obscured by the surrounding trees. But that was more than enough time. We could all see small orange flames on the roof of the wooden building.

"Sons of bitches," Buster growled, stretching his words out in a vengeful, hateful tone. "They did it, Pa! They fucking did it!"

"Look! There's a car!" I blurted out. "See it? See the red tail lights? It's pulling away from the store."

"I see them!" said Fred Sampson. "It's too damn far and dark to tell what kind of a car it is. But it is definitely a car, not a truck."

"Yeah, the bastard's heading south," Buster added, as the two red lights and the store disappeared behind the tree line.

Jerking his head back toward the windshield Buster goosed the throttle and we sped straight toward the dock. Only a couple of minutes passed before he brought her down off plane, but when he did we were approaching the wooden structure too fast. Slam! *The Island Belle* rammed into a piling. The boat jolted hard and, at the exact same moment, ear-splitting thunder boomed directly overhead, again. The storm had caught up with us. Thin streaks of erratic, white lightning scratched the clouds, but it didn't stop Fred. Lickity-split, like a cat, he was up on the bow tying a line to the dock.

Now shifting the big engines from reverse into neutral, Buster told Pa to finish tying her up. The current was already pulling the stern away from the berth, but there was no time to dillydally with that. Buster, Fred and I leapt off the bow onto the dock, and when we hit the wooden planking Fred let out a howl. "Ohhhh shit! That hurts!" Wearing just flip-flops he'd landed on his left ankle with all his weight. His foot had broken through the thong on the rubber sandal and two huge splinters spiked into his foot when it slid. Buster and I paused to take a look but Fred blurted, "Forget about me. Get the hell down to the store, quick!

Buster and I raced off the dock, rounded the cistern alongside the house then kept going across the lawn and into the jungle. As we dodged trees and bushes in the blackness, I felt all kinds of unknown things crunching beneath my feet. There was no stopping. We had to get to that store before the fire got totally out of hand. Then, just as we reached the curve in the shell road, it started to rain. It poured.

Big, heavy drops started beating the palmettos and trees all around us. I could smell the musky scent of the woods as a black crowned night heron protested our arrival. "Kwawk" it cried out from somewhere in the dark woods as we pushed through the heaven-sent tropical downpour. We didn't take the road. Instead Buster said, "This way!", and led me through a shortcut. Side by side, with rain dripping off the bill of his cap and streaming down my face, we dashed through a stand of pines, slipping and sliding on a soaking wet bed of dead pine needles.

There had been two separate fires set at the back of the building. The first one had climbed up the wall of the convenience store; the other, thirty feet down, behind the bar. Both were started on the outside, *after* the back wall had been doused with gasoline. The good news was that it hadn't gotten out of hand. By the time Buster and I came huffing and puffing up to the building, the windblown, pelting rain had all but extinguished the flames. And it was still coming down hard as ever.

"Thank God!" I said as we both bent over, hands on hips, trying to catch our breath.

"Yeah," Buster came back. "A little longer and she would have burned clear through the wall."

To his right, leaning against the back door, there was a mop sticking out of a bucket that had overflowed with rain water. He picked it up and started ramming the handle into the scorched areas of the wall.

"None of it burnt through," he said. "Probably won't have to replace any of this – just clean it up and paint it."

"I guess there's no sense in calling the fire department now," I said, as if asking a question.

"Hell no, every time them fire inspectors come by, we pass by the skin of our teeth. Don't want to give 'em an excuse to close us up."

"How old is the building?" I asked, with dripping strands of brown hair hanging over my eyes.

"My great granddaddy built it before the Civil War," he said, putting the mop head back into the bucket. "Was a small church back then. Folks used to come over from Big Pine by boat every Sunday for services."

"And, now it's a bar."

"Yeah, Ma never liked the idea, her bein' sort of religious. C'mon, let's take a look at where the other fire was and then go inside."

That fire was even less damaging than the first; so after spitting a stream of tobacco juice Buster unlocked the padlocked back door to the bar and we stepped inside. The place smelled like the usual barroom bouquet of cigarettes, the previous night's beer, and pine cleaner. Buster stepped along the back wall where some pictures and stuffed fish hung. Pushing the overlapping wooden boards with his herculean strength, nothing gave. It seemed everything was still solid.

"Looks like that rain got here in a nick of time," he said.

"Yeah, everything seems okay in here!"

"Yupper. Let's check the store."

Everything was shipshape in there as well. Satisfied with what we'd seen after poking around a few minutes, Buster was locking up just as Pa came up the road. It wasn't raining anymore. The storm had dissipated and what was left of it moved on to the south.

"You put it all out?" Pa asked his son.

"The rain did. Everything's alright. Come here."

We then stepped around to the back again and Buster showed Pa the burn marks on the wall.

As Pa assessed the damage his old face looked both sad and angry.

"Yep," he said, "some sumbitch started it alright. This ain't no accident."

"Are you going to call the sheriff?" I asked.

"Naw," Pa said, standing there all glassy-eyed now. "Ain't nothin' *they* can do. We'll find out who did it. Then we'll take care of it our own way."

I didn't like hearing Pa talk that way. He and Buster were good people. They didn't deserve something like this. I had no idea how they might retaliate but wasn't about to ask. It was none of my business. Pa had said they'd take care of it their way, and I was sure he and Buster were already conjuring some ideas. That bothered me. From what Julie had told me the day before, I well knew that going up against Lionel Topper and his crowd could be very risky business.

Before we left we searched in the darkness for clues but came up empty.

"Let's call it a night," Buster finally said. "I gotta clean up the boat and get some shut-eye."

"I'll give you a hand," I said, then turned to Pa and asked him, "What about Fred? How's he doing?"

"When I left, Jackie was pullin' two nasty splinters out his foot. I'm gonna check on him when we get back, but I'm sure he'll be fine. C'mon, let's get goin'."

The three of us sloshed through the puddles back there and came out at the corner of the building.

That's when I noticed something lying beneath a palmetto bush just off to the side.

"Hold on," I said, as I stepped over to it and picked it up. "It's a matchbook! Says Hugs and Jugs, Key West Florida. Julie just told me yesterday that when she was at work a few days ago Topper and some friends of his had stopped in for drinks. She overheard them say they were going to Hugs and Jugs when they were leaving."

"We know," Buster said as he came alongside me. "Julie told us all about it. Here, let me see it."

Buster opened it up. It was empty. All the matches had been ripped out.

"Hmmm," he said, "ain't no wear on this. It's soaked, like everything else, but the colors ain't the least bit faded."

He then closed the cover and we studied for a few seconds. The resolution of the pink lettering on the glossy, black background was still perfect.

"It ain't been here for long," Pa said. "It definitely was either Topper or one of his flunkies who started the fires. And I'll tell ya another thing. When we saw those taillights from the boat, I noticed the left one looked brighter than the right."

"I thought the same thing," I said, "but it was so far away I couldn't be sure. You must have good eyes,

Pa."

"Not really. The binoculars were lying in front of me at the time. I picked 'em up real quick like and got a look just before the bastard was out of sight."

"Ya see anything else," Buster asked.

"Nope. That was it. Woulda told you by now if I did."

"It ain't much to go on," Buster said, squeezing the matchbook as if he were trying to get even with it, "but it's a start. I'm gonna be doing some snooping around real soon."

I don't know what made me say what I did next, then again, I do. I genuinely liked these guys and everybody else on the key. Not only that, but I'd always had a disdain for Lionel Topper types. I'd been rooting for underdogs all my life. And though I'd never seen many of them win during my thirty-nine years on this planet, that only made me pull all the harder for them now.

"Buster," I said, "if you're going to check that Hugs and Jugs place out, I want to go with you."

Lowering his head; narrowing his eyes, I could tell he was giving me a chance to reconsider, "You sure about that?"

"I'm in. When do you want to go?"

“Meet you here in the bar, ’bout eight tomorrow night. We’re all pretty ragged out right now.”

After we tromped back to the dock, I noticed Pa’s forehead had pulled into creases. He was tired, and damned concerned about all that had happened. When we were about halfway back, he warned Buster, “When you go down to Key West tomorrow, I don’t want you turnin’ the whole damn town upside down.”

“Nah. Don’t worry about nothin’.”

“Yeah, sure! Don’t worry about nothing! Just like when you went down lookin’ for that guy who got weird with Sissy at the store that time. I don’t want to be bailin’ you outta jail again.”

I didn’t know a thing about the incident Pa had mentioned, but I did now know that as nice a guy as Buster was, he had a temper.

The three of us cleaned up the boat quickly and then called it a night. The heavy downpour had rinsed any salt spray from the evening’s trip so the cleanup was a snap. Even though it was obvious that Fred and Jackie had managed to get to their trailers, I volunteered to stop at their places and let them know that everything was okay at the store. The light was out at Jackie’s so I went over to Fred’s. They were both there. Fred had taped Jackie’s ankle, which by then had swelled to the size of a softball.

“It’ll be fine in a few days. It’s just a sprain,” said Jackie, who had administered plenty of first aid during his years on the N.Y.P.D.

I only stayed a few minutes. After giving them a quick rundown about the condition of the store and what we suspected, I trudged back to the Airstream to get some much-needed rest. It had been a long night. And I worried that the next might be even longer.

Chapter 12

The following evening I left a half hour early to meet Buster at Barnacle Bell's. Antsy as I was, I just had to get out of that trailer. Hour after hour, all day long, my mind had been whirling round and round like a gulf water spout. And it still was. Time and again I'd envisioned a hundred different possible outcomes of this trip to Key West. And none were promising.

There were quite a few vehicles parked outside the bar when I arrived, but as soon as I stepped inside Pa saw me and fished a Miller Lite from the cooler. As I approached a vacant stool he twisted the cap off, wiped the top of the bottle with his fresh apron, and said, "Sorry Sonny, these Millers could be a wee bit colder."

"That's fine, as long as it's wet. Looks like it's business as usual here, huh?" I said, glancing around at the goodly crowd of customers, then at the back wall – right about where it had been burned on the outside. Relieved for the second time that there'd been no damage, I then turned my head back around, laid a ten on the bar and picked up the beer bottle standing before me. In a quick succession of gulps I emptied half is contents. Pa watched me warily, saying nothing. But as soon as I plunked the bottle back on the bar he said, "Now don't be gettin' too fired up. You just might need to have your wits about you later."

"No problem. I'll be okay," I said. But I had one foot resting on the brass foot rail that encircled the bar, and the knee just up from it was pumping up and down like a piston. I caught myself and held it still.

Pa stepped away to wait on some other customers and by the time he came back I'd emptied the beer.

"Want another?" he asked, holding up the bottle.

"I'm going to do a pitcher instead."

Swiveling his head to the side, Pa studied me from the corners of his knowing eyes for one short moment. Satisfied that I'd gotten his message, he then reached for a pitcher, put it beneath a tap and let a cold yellow stream flow into it.

"You're a big boy. I guess you know what you're doin'."

Once the glass pitcher was filled he sat it and an empty glass in front of me then walked to the other side of the bar to serve a group of sunburnt construction workers. All of them had their ball caps turned backwards and seemed to be feeling little or no pain. Loud but not quite boisterous yet, they were hitting on two grocery store cashiers. One of the women, a redhead with the top of her powder blue uniform unbuttoned low enough to expose a generous portion of two freckled breasts, was eye to eye with one of the wood butchers. He said something to her that I couldn't hear, but I did hear her comeback. Smiling seductively, ever so slowly running her index finger down her cleavage, she said in a deep throaty voice, "How'd you like to find out?" On the ring finger of the same hand she was enticing him with there was a cheap gold band. But it didn't seem to bother either one of them. She picked her purse up from the bar, whispered something to her friend, and they were out of there.

I swiveled around and watched them through the front window for a moment. As the two locked arms around each other and leaned against the guy's green, sun-faded pickup, all I could think of was Wendy and Steve Silverman. I felt like another piece of my heart was being wrenched off. As much as I'd thought I was over her, it still hurt. I felt that dark, all too familiar funk settling in again. But then I got lucky.

Before the gloom could completely shroud my spirit there was a distraction. I saw Julie on the other side of the glass. She was walking toward the door, about to come into the bar. The clown with the backwards hat – class act that he was, ogled at her. Exposing a set of nasty looking teeth, he smiled and said something to Julie, but she just kept walking. As bad-teeth's new girlfriend gave him a playful slap, they shared a boozed-up laugh and climbed into the truck.

Julie came through the doorway along with the

last of the day's sunlight. Looking like royalty in cutoffs, we exchanged hellos then she alighted onto the stool next to me.

"What'll ya have, Julie?' Pa asked, as she crossed her long legs elegantly beneath the bar.

"Just a Coke Pa. Sissy and I have to do some studying tonight."

Tapping the bills lying on the bar in front of me, I said, "I've got it Pa." Then I turned back to Julie. "You're going to be darn sure she passes that GED, aren't you?"

Nodding her head she said, "She's going for her test on Wednesday."

"Is she coming along okay?"

"Sure, she's an extremely bright kid. Her retention abilities are remarkable."

"She sure seems very sharp." I said before lowering my voice, looking around the bar, and adding, "I guess you heard all about the fire?"

"I sure did. And I think we all know who's responsible. But let me ask you something. What do you and Buster think you're going to accomplish tonight?"

"I don't know ... proof, I guess. We're hoping to

get some proof that Topper was behind it. Then we'll take it from there." My knee was bouncing again, both of them were.

"You know how dangerous this thing can get, don't you Sonny?" Julie said, looking deep inside my eyes the way she did when she was very serious.

"I know! I know! Believe me I've given it a lot of thought."

"Then why are you guys going?"

"Like I said, to get to the bottom of this thing."

I lit a cigarette, inhaled it then went on, "I don't have a vested interest in this island or anything like that. But I like it here. And I like the people, too. I've seen the little guys bullied around all my life, so in a way it does concern me. I'm not going to sit back and just watch."

Someone had fed the juke box and the old Beatles' hit, *It Don't Come Easy*, reverberated throughout the bar. Julie had to raise her voice a bit when she said, "I can appreciate you feeling that way. But why can't you guys just get the police to handle it?"

"Because they'd surely send the fire department here to investigate the fire. Buster said the place barely passes its fire inspection every year because of the age of the building."

Julie thought aloud, "I see. They would shut Pa down."

"Believe me ... I'm not looking forward to this," I said, pouring myself another glass of beer.

"Just don't get too courageous."

"I know. I know."

Julie studied her Coke for a moment. She swirled the glass around a couple of times then said, "I wonder where Jackie and Fred are."

"Fred had a late afternoon doctor's appointment up in Marathon. It wasn't easy, but I talked him into going up to Fisherman's Hospital for x-rays."

"They're still there?"

"You know how those two are. They said they'd probably make the rounds up there after the x-rays. Jackie said he likes the karaoke at one of the places there. I think he said the Hurricane ... yeah, that's it, the Hurricane Lounge."

Right about then the entrance door opened again, and Julie shifted her eyes over her shoulder. It was Buster. It was the first time I'd seen him without his Redman cap perched on his head. With his hair combed neatly, he put me to mind of a giant schoolboy – a giant *unhappy* schoolboy.

"My, don't we look all spiffy?" Julie said, smiling now.

"Yeah," I chimed in, "you lost the hat?"

"All right, all right," Buster came back in his usual deep, resonate voice. "Don't be givin' me a bad time now."

Holding my glass up now, I asked him, "Are you going to have a couple?"

"No, I'm okay. I wanna git into this one straight, but I've got a couple of cold ones in the truck if you want 'em."

"Well ... I'm ready if you are," I said, with the words feeling just the slightest bit clumsy as they came out.

I stood up, emptied my glass and glanced at the pitcher. It was already two-thirds empty. I shook my head and picked my cigarettes up from the bar as Julie got out of her seat as well. Pa stopped rinsing glasses for a moment from his post behind the bar and told us to be very careful.

When we stepped outside into the sticky Florida evening, a Greyhound bus lit us up with its lights before it roared by. Once it had passed Julie's beautiful face winced when she said, "Be careful, you two. Please."

Moments later, with Buster steering his Ford pickup down the Overseas Highway, I turned to look out the back window. Julie was still standing in the dark parking lot. She was watching us, and she continued to until we rounded a curve and drove out of sight.

Chapter 13

"Beer's in there." Buster said, nodding at a small cooler between us on the floorboard.

"No thanks," I told him, "I'm alright for now."

We didn't say anything else for the next mile or two. It's very dark at night in the lower reaches of the Florida Keys, and there were virtually no lights along the stretch of highway we were on. Not many cars either. My mind only drifted as I peered into the surrounding blackness.

When we drove through Summerland Key, Buster honked at a couple of friends – good old boys, coming out of an isolated convenience store. Both of them were toting twelve-packs of Old Milwaukee but when they recognized Buster's truck they each raised a hand in a slow wave. Nobody hurries in the Keys, only the tourists who are either just arriving or just leaving.

Before I knew it, we were crossing the inky waters of Boca Chica Channel and coming onto Stock Island.

"See that big ole bar comin' up on the left?" Buster asked.

"Yeah."

"That is one wild and crazy place, man. Plenty

rough too. It's called The Purple Conch."

As we passed it, two angry men were out in front shouting in each other's faces. A frazzled looking woman in a white tee shirt down to her knees was trying to get between the two. She was one feisty lady though. With a drink glass and cigarette in one hand, she was shoving the two combatants with the other. She was doing it pretty damn hard too. It was an intense confrontation for sure. The whole scenario, painted purple by a neon sign across the top of the austere, cement-block building, only seemed to add to the drama.

"That reminds me of my wilder days back in New York, before I got married," I said to Buster.

"Is that what brought you down this way ... " he asked as he down shifted the gears for a red light, "a busted up marriage?"

"Yeah," I said, and as I continued I heard each of my words echo in the emptiness inside me, "seventeen years with the same woman. Then, one day, I found out that after all that time I couldn't trust her anymore. Now there isn't much of anything I trust."

Buster said nothing as he hung a right onto North Roosevelt, and I just watched the small waves of Key West Harbor as they danced in the glowing light of the business district. A short distance later Buster turned a fast, hard left across the boulevard into the parking lot of Hugs & Jugs, just beating a barrage of oncoming headlights. The driver of the closest car leaned on his horn angrily as he passed by. It was a rushed, impulsive decision that I wouldn't have expected Buster to make; way out of character for a man who normally took things slow and easy.

As soon as we entered the crowded parking lot we slowly motored around the lighted image of a fifteen-foot female dancer. A tall, pink neon Amazon she was; gyrating enticingly atop a high, metal post. With light dancing on the hood of Buster's pickup, he drove around it and parked right next to the wild lady, facing the boulevard. Hearing the sign buzzing and the sound of insects popping on hot tubular glass, I asked Buster as we climbed out, "We want to lock it up here, don't we?"

"You bet we do!" was his answer.

Inside the joint there was all kinds of hooting and hollering going on. Every type of psyched-up, boozed-up, horned-up male you can think of was in there. Sailors, drifters, business types, rednecks, tourists, pirates, villains and more were crowded around the sprawling bar and sitting at tables. Half of them were shouting words of encouragement to a dancer as she strutted her stuff on stage-like platform in back. All was dark except for some strobe lights that pulsated across the tall, scantly-covered blonde. I could see she had a tough edge to her face, but her body was shapely and she knew how to flaunt it. As she shimmied, bounced and jounced her goods to the Stones' hit *Start Me Up,* Buster and I walked along the front of the place to an empty table by a window. Perfect. It looked right out into the parking lot.

As soon as we sat down, I lit a cigarette from a red-globed candle on the table and a waitress appeared. She seemed nervous as hell and didn't look a day over sixteen. Sam bam she took our order and disappeared as quickly as she had arrived. I felt bad for the kid. With the expression on her face and the bashful look in her eyes, you didn't have to be a genius to see that she did not want to be there for another minute. When she returned with two beers Buster and I both gave her a nice tip. We could have waited until we were about to leave but wanted to cheer her up a bit. She did manage a small smile but then went right back to her drudgery.

Buster and I each took a swallow of cold beer then glanced at the dancer. She had slowed the pace for a moment as two men took turns inserting bills in the string of her G. That was more than fine with her. But then another guy approached her. He looked like trouble. Resembling a long-haired James Dean but with a tattoo banded around his biceps, he wasn't all smiles like the first two who'd made donations to the dancer's cause. No, this guy had a pouty look about him, a *cocky* pouty look. And when he inserted his money, he didn't just put it beneath the string that encircled her waist. He just *had* to put the bill inside the patch of red silky material in front of the G-string. The smile the blonde had been wearing quickly left her face, yet it looked as if she was going to let the nervy gesture go. But then Mister Dean let his fingers linger in there far longer than he should have. That's when she lost it.

Taking one step back with her right foot the long-legged woman quickly snapped it forward, right smack into Mr. Dean's face. It was nasty. His head snapped back and immediately blood oozed out of both nostrils. She swung her leg so hard that even after making contact her high-heeled foot lifted way up past her head.

The rowdy mob whistled and cheered, but the guy who got kicked didn't think it was the least bit entertaining. He wiped his nose with his hand, looked at it, then leaped right up onto the stage. Retreating now, the dancer took two quick steps backward. But that didn't matter. She was safe. For as quickly as the bad actor had jumped up, two burly bouncers emerged from the crowd. And they didn't fool around. Each of them grabbed one of the guy's ankles and they both yanked at the same time. The bad actor went straight down – face-first onto the stage. There was even more blood now. It splattered everywhere. But that didn't faze the two housemen in the least. Nonchalantly, as if this kind of thing happened every fifteen minutes, they dragged the squirming, kicking, screaming man all the way to the front door. Once there they calmly opened it up, deposited him onto Roosevelt Boulevard, and returned to their posts inside. Not a word had been spoken between them. It was business as usual.

"Whoosh, that was bad," I said to Buster. "Did you see her kick?"

"Sure did. If his head was a football it would have gone fifty yards."

"This is one great place." I said cynically.

"Yeah, I hear ya. I've only been in here two or three times before ... and only because I happened to be rip-roarin' drunk."

"I can see why," I said as I checked out some of the shadier characters sitting and standing in the nearly dark establishment. "They've got a lovely clientele."

Buster scoped out the crowd also but didn't see any of Topper's crowd. After that, his head snapped toward that window every time another car pulled into the parking lot. He must have looked out there fifteen times in as many minutes. He was hoping to spot a car with one dim taillight.

"Buster," I finally said, "you know this is a long shot."

"Yeah, I know. But that matchbook and a dim

right-side taillight are all we've got to go on right now."

A minute or so later, two more men entered the bar. It was Cap Forest and Dalton Judge. Cap's stern face appeared a little looser than usual so I figured the two of them had been making the rounds. I stood up and flagged them over to the table just as a new dancer hopped onto the stage. A light-skinned black girl, with white features, she instantly went into her routine when the DJ blasted Madonna's *Material Girl* so loud it sounded like a boom box in a closet.

"Hey Boss! Dalton! Over here!" I said, standing up and waving them over.

"How you boys doin'?" Cap mumbled without removing the Doral cigarette from his lips. Then, leaning over to shake Buster's hand, he said, "Long time no see."

"I've been okay. How 'bout yourself?"

"Gettin' by," Cap said as he and Dalton plopped down on chairs.

"I've been meanin' to get up to the shop," Buster said, "but ain't got around to it. Need to stock up on some tackle and get you to replace some drag washers in my trollin' reels."

"I'll get my Yankee here to replace 'em," Forest said, actually allowing himself a smile when he looked my way. There was a hint of fondness in the good-natured remark, and I appreciated that, but I could also tell he'd already had more than a few swigs from that flask he always carried.

"Oh yeah," Forest then said, pushing a rogue strand of hair out of his eyes, "this here's Dalton Judge, Buster. And Dalton, this is Buster Bell."

"Good to meet ya," Dalton said.

After the two men shook hands and exchanged a few words, Cap tapped a passing waitress on the elbow and ordered two Johnnie Walker Red's with beer chasers. Then he said to Buster, "Sonny told me you had a little trouble down there on Wrecker's Key last night."

"Yeah, we had trouble alright," he said, twisting his beer bottle in little quarter turns on the table, looking at Dalton Judge now.

"You don't have to worry about Dalton," Cap said immediately. "He's good people."

"Well, like Sonny probably told ya, we were lucky. Got there `bout five minutes after the fire was set. A cloud opened up and all but doused it by the time we got there."

"Any idea who'd want to do somethin' like that?" Cap asked.

"Yeah, I got an idea."

"Who?"

"You ever heard of some rich-assed developer name of Topper?"

"Yeah," said Cap Forest, "I sure have – *Lionel* Topper. Matter of fact that sumbitch just happened to be in here last night. Let me think what time he ... "

"It was right kinda late, right about eleven," Dalton Judge interrupted. "He came in with three others just like him – business types."

"That's right," Cap said, lifting his dark eyebrows, "and about ten minutes later who walks in and sits with them but Brock Blackburn. You know him?"

"No. But I've heard stories about him."

"Well, I guarantee ya everything you've heard about him is true, probably worse. Anyway, he walks over to Topper's table and Topper gets all nervous looking. He's lookin' all around as if he don't want to be seen with Blackburn. He got out of his chair real quick after that and the two of them went outside."

"Yeah," Dalton said. "Then a few minutes later Topper came back in alone. He sat back down with his buddies and, real secretive like, told them something. They all were leaning over their table, real close together like they were in a football huddle, and just as they straightened back up in their chairs, Brock Blackburn came back in." Dalton stopped there for a second and jerked his thumb toward the club's farthest wall before adding, "He went straight to that itty bitty auxiliary bar way over there, hammered down a few quickies, and then left."

"Yeah," Cap said, "and we weren't far behind him. That's how I know Dalton was right about Topper getting' here at around eleven. We walked outta here right after Blackburn did, and I got home at ten after midnight. I know 'cause Maggie gave me holy hell when I got there."

"What's this Blackburn character look like?" Buster asked then. "And where's he live?"

"`He lives in a trailer ... on Stock Island somewhere," Cap said, looking more than a little tipsy by then. "He's 'bout your size, Buster, maybe a bit taller even, with black hair almost down to his ass. Wears it all combed back, like a wild man. Muscular sumbitch too! I used to see him around when I was doin' time in Raiford."

Cap took another long swig of beer; glanced inside the bottle for god knows what, and raised his eyes back up at Buster's. "You'll know Blackburn if you see him. He's got a gold ring on one ear and four tattooed teardrops falling from his left eye. Do ya know what them teardrops mean, Buster?"

"No."

“I think I know,” I said, trying to fight off the look of dread that was forcing itself on my face. “Go ahead, tell us.”

“One tear means the person wearin’ it has killed at least one person.”

God knows what four signifies! I thought, my knees now bouncing for the second time that night.

“Blackburn got the tats in Raiford,” Cap slurred now. “We had an ink slinger they called `Hard Time’ – a black guy, a lifer who was locked up for a triple murder. He made this tattooing machine from a tiny *Walkman* motor and bits of guitar strings. Anyway, the general consensus of the population up there was that Blackburn didn’t like his art work. Because the day after Hard Time did Blackburn’s teardrops, the screws found him in a pile of dirty laundry – deader ’n shit. His neck was snapped and he had 18 stab wounds in his chest, back, and face. I saw him when they drug his body from that laundry pile, nothin’ but butchered black meat marinated in blood. And the words Payback’s a bitch’ were tattooed across his forehead.”

Cap’s head was getting heavy by now. It was plain to see he was fighting to support it. “Hard Time only gave Blackburn three tears that night. Two days later, ’e had a fourth one. And it wasn’t blue like the others; it was black. Even the guards didn’t ask no questions.”

"This guy sounds like a regular prince," I said, silently questioning my involvement in this mess more than ever. *Am I going to get myself killed over this? Maybe I better bow the hell out of this mess, before it's too late.*

"You know what he drives?" Buster asked.

"A beat-up Chevy pickup – burgundy," Dalton said, turning his head toward the window and nodding at it. "We watched him pull out of the lot last night."

"Alright, guys. Thanks," Buster said. "You ready to go, Sonny?"

As we got up to leave, Cap gave us one more bit of information. Slurring his words by then he said, "Oh yeah, I almost forgot to tell ya something. When I was up in Raiford, Blackburn was in that time for arson. Word was he's got a thing for fire. Sumbitch likes to play with matches."

Chapter 14

Neither Buster nor I said much during the drive back to Wrecker's Key. We were both too deep in our thoughts. Sitting there with the warm, night air rumbling through my open window, I knew that he was working out a plan of action. As for myself, I was ashamed of what I was thinking. I wanted out. Over and over I tried to find just the right words to tell Buster. No matter which words came to mind or how I arranged them, none if it seemed right. Finally, as if Buster was in this mess by himself now, I broke the silence saying, "What are *you* going to do about this guy, Buster?"

He remained silent for another few moments. He didn't even look at me, but I watched his intent face. In the dim white glow of the dashboard I could see lines and creases that normally weren't in his face. Finally, he turned to me and said, "I don't know yet."

"Maybe we better bring the cops in on this one."

Shaking his head, his voice laced with both disappointment in me and anger at all the rest, he said, "That's not how we do things down here." Then he turned back to the road and silently drove on.

For the first time since I arrived on Wreckers, I felt alienated. I was wiggling my way out of a tight spot and hated myself for it. I wanted to tell Buster that I'd be with him all the way, but I didn't. Instead I lit a cigarette, exhaled the smoke out the open window, and watched it dissipate in the night – along with Buster's earlier perception of me.

The next morning I rose to the clock radio like I always did. But lying in bed with my eyes open, I didn't even see the ceiling above me. I was too deep in thought. And those first thoughts were the exact same as the previous night's last – how I had disappointed Buster. It was the first morning since coming to Florida that I didn't hop right out of bed. I couldn't. My cowardice was eating at me too ferociously, and I again felt that nagging hollowness inside. This was the second time that I considered packing it in and leaving Wreckers Key.

Where will I go? I've got even less money behind me than when I first came down here. Maybe I should head up to Atlanta ... look for a real job again. No! I don't think so.

I was falling in love with my new home *and* the alternative lifestyle I was living. Up until the night before, I'd felt like I belonged. The tropical keys were breathtaking. The warm, gentle climate and slow pace were helping me get reacquainted with my soul. I had calmed down considerably, driving slower and biting my fingernails less. Every time I looked out at the sparkling, turquoise ocean, I felt new hope and promise. I just couldn't bring myself to leave.

I wanted to go after that Blackburn character with Buster, but this was a serious situation – possibly deadly serious. What would a lunatic like Blackburn do when we confronted him about the fire, just sit there and apologize? What's he going to say, I'm so sorry, I won't do it again? Was he going to break down and confess that Lionel Topper made him do it? No, that wasn't going to happen. Brock Blackburn was a murderer, several times over. And what the hell was I going to do, shoot him?

As I got ready for work and later when I drove there, similar heavy thoughts preoccupied my mind. It wasn't until I pulled into the parking area at Big Time Bait and Tackle that all that troublesome clutter cleared out of my head. Just a few minutes after seven and already there were customers waiting by the front door. I parked the van, unlocked the door and immediately serviced the three customers. As soon as they left, I put on a pot of coffee then turned on the VHF radio. After listening to a couple of charter boat captains squawking to each other for a few minutes, I heard Cap Forest's tired voice reporting to another guide named J.D. Wells.

"We already boated a big ole cuda and a wahoo about thirty pounds."

J.D. then asked him where he was fishing and I could hear Cap exhaling smoke with his answer, "We're out over the Santa Maria wreck, and I'm on top of a ton of fish."

The skippers always communicated in cryptic jargon when secretive information was being discussed. They had bogus names for certain hotspots they used amongst themselves. Doing so prevented any outsiders who might be listening from identifying where they were fishing. This way no strangers could crowd in on whoever was doing the talking. Fat chance the eavesdroppers would ever find the nonexistent Santa Maria wreck.

"That Cap freaking amazes me." I said aloud to myself. "After the condition he was in last night, how in god's name did he ever make it out on the water so early?"

Then it dawned on me. Certainly he did it with the help of his Jack Daniels flask.

I then walked to the tiny backroom and sure enough, the army cot was opened. An ashtray full of butts sat on the floor next to it and one had smoldered all the way to the filter. It was surely the previous evenings last. There were three empty cans of Busch beer strewn on the floor and one standing upright. It was half full of warm, stale beer. Obviously, Cap hadn't made it home to Maggie. I figured that was just as well.

I folded up the canvas cot and trashed the beer cans after emptying the full one in the weeds outside the back door. When I stepped back inside someone came into the store. It was Julie, and I was genuinely surprised

"Hello, Sonny."

"Hi! How are you?"

"Smells like an ocean in here," she said, as she peeked into the shrimp tank, picked up the short-handled net, and extracted a couple of jumping, snapping shrimp. After studying them for a moment she put them back in the water and turned to me.

"Coffee?" I asked, raising my foam cup.

"No thanks, I'm good. Buster's already out on *The Island Belle*, and I couldn't wait to find out how last night went, so I thought I'd drive up here."

She was trying to camouflage her concern by fiddling with the shrimp, but I could see it all over her face. Nevertheless, I was flattered that she was so worried.

"Nothing really," I said, as I picked at one of my short fingernails. Full of self-disdain after letting Buster down the night before, my heart still pumping shame through all my arteries, I weakly added, "We think we know who did it, though."

Julie`s concerned eyes narrowed even more now. Tilting her head forward, waiting as if commanding my eyes to meet hers, she asked, "Who was it?"

"We're all but positive it was Brock Blackburn. Cap Forest told us last night that he did prison time with him. He told us a few more things too."

"Who's Cap Forest?"

"My boss – the owner of this shop."

"What makes you think Blackburn did it?"

"Cap saw him meet with Lionel Topper at a Key West strip joint Thursday night; shortly after the fire was set."

"So?" Julie said, still clinging to the hope that Blackburn possibly didn't start the fire.

"What do you mean – so? You know this guy isn't one of the champagne and brunch bunch. Believe me, he's not the type a guy like Topper would want to be seen with in public, if he didn't have to. As soon as Blackburn, who by the way has teardrops tattooed on his face, came in, Topper jumped up from his table and ushered him outside – pronto. As you know, this maniac has *murdered* people! On top of that, we found out last night that he's got a fire fetish. He likes playing with matches."

"I don't like this, Sonny. I don't like any of it."

"Hell," I snapped, "you think *I* like it?"

Julie chewed her upper lip and said nothing. She

looked hurt. In the silence that followed, the steady hiss of aerators spraying water into the shrimp tank seemed deafening.

Finally, trying to cut through the tension, my voice cracked when I said, “I’m sorry, Julie. It’s just that ... well, I feel like I’m hanging Buster up.”

“Why?” she asked gently, as she sat on the wooden stool in front of the counter. “What happened?”

“Oh, it was on the way home last night. I asked him what *he* was going to do about Topper and the lunatic – not what *we* were going to do. I was backing out.”

“Hmmm ... the macho thing. Sonny, I don’t think you were a bit wrong. This isn’t something either of you should handle. You’ve got to let the sheriff’s department take care of this. Neither of you need to get involved with this ... this killer.”

“You know that people like Buster and Pa don’t go to the police with their problems. And, I can’t say that I blame them. There’s no hard evidence, but we know who did it. There’s not much room for doubt.”

“So, what does Buster plan on doing?”

“I asked him. He said he didn’t know yet.”

“That’s not good,” Julie said. Then, realizing

she'd just laid her left hand on the counter top, she quickly withdrew it before I could see it. She put it behind her back and started fumbling as if she were tucking her tank top into the back of her white shorts.

Right then and there I wanted to apologize for the way I'd acted the morning after our affair. But I didn't. I thought it best to let it go for the time being. I'd known all along that Julie was special, but only recently I'd begun to realize that it just might be possible something could come of our relationship. But it was only that – a possibility. Yes, she truly cared for me. I read that loud and clear. But I needed to work things out in my head and in my heart. First I needed to truly convince myself that I could make a go of it with her. I would never say anything until I was totally sure. I didn't want to hurt her again. This wasn't the time or place, anyway. And I now had far more pressing things whirling through my head and weighing heavy on my shoulders. I wanted in the worst way to help Buster out, but I could very well end up getting myself killed.

"Julie," I said in a desperate, agitated tone now, "what do *you* suggest I do? I can't just walk up to Buster and tell him he can't deal with this maniac."

I then glanced out the front window and said in a softer voice, "Here come some customers."

"You get off at five, right?" Julie asked quickly.

"Yes."

I was surprised she knew my schedule.

"Come to my trailer. I'll make dinner for you."

Before I could answer either way she spun around and walked away. As she passed by the two customers; a couple of yahoos, they stopped, turned, and ogled at her behind.

"That's what I call a real woman," one of the yokels muttered to the other, obviously not too concerned with subtleness. "That one I got at home ain't nothin' like that!"

I wanted to slap him up against his dense head. But I didn't.

The rest of the day crawled like they always do during summertime in the tropics. Only on the few occasions when several customers came into the shop at once did time seem to speed up. I'd go an hour or so without a single customer coming in and then, as if I'd put a sign out by the road saying I was giving everything away, a batch of vehicles would pull into the marl parking lot all at once. The place would become abuzz with conversations as patrons bragged, exaggerated, and lied to one another about their fishing conquests. Then, just as quickly as the store had come alive, all would be quiet again. Left alone once again with only that hissing shrimp tank and the

VHF, my thoughts would bounce from Julie to Blackburn to Buster to Topper and back again. All day long I tried to come up with solutions. But it didn't happen. There was just no way I could draw any conclusions with my mind spinning the way it was.

Eventually, five o'clock rolled around and Maggie relieved me. I got out of there like right now. I climbed into the van, wore the sulphur off several humid matches before one ignited, lit my sixth smoke of the day then pulled out onto The Overseas Highway. In just a matter of minutes I was approaching the Wrecker's Key Bridge, and I did not like what I saw there.

The entire expanse of Lionel Topper's *Flagler Colony Resort* property had been bordered along the road with new wooden survey stakes. There were red plastic strips tied to the tops of each of them, and the way they were snapping in the southerly breeze I felt as if they were taunting me, threatening me, daring me to get involved in the dangerous mess again.

Some trees scattered throughout the property had the same red ribbons tied around their trunks. Mostly Australian pines and tall, stately palm trees, they would obviously be spared from the destructive bulldozers. Perusing the whole scene as I slowed down, I could see that half the island had been cordoned off. Acres and acres of saw palmettos, sandspurs, snakes, and coons had been surrounded by the wooden sticks. I hadn't realized the devastating breadth of Topper's project until now. All I could do was shake my head.

After crossing the bridge, I hung a right just before the old wooden sign and pulled in front of Pa's store. Sissy was seated behind the counter, but it wasn't until the screen door squeaked closed behind me that she raised her eyes from behind a textbook. With all I had on my mind, and being more than a little nervous about being alone with Julie again, I certainly didn't feel like dealing with Sissy. But I didn't have a choice. There was something I *had* to buy.

"Hi," I said, feeling like a nervy intruder.

As if being held at gunpoint, she grudgingly said hello. Then she immediately planted her nose back behind her history book.

Figuring the heck with her, I headed toward the back of the store but didn't get very far. I hadn't taken two full steps before she said in that same disinterested tone, "Wine's in the back cooler ... next to the beer."

"How'd you know I wanted wine?" I asked, turning back around.

She still wouldn't look at me. Without raising her eyes she said matter-of-factly, "A guy goes to a lady's house for dinner, he should bring something."

I tramped to the back of the store and yanked a bottle of Yago Sant' Gria from the wall cooler. I was getting more and more tired of Sissy's treatment every time I saw her. I didn't know whether to sail into her right then and get it over with or to let it ride. Lately, I hadn't been sure about anything.

Back up front I clunked the bottle on the counter and snapped, "I want a pack of Carlton 100's, too." I extracted a ten from my wallet and put it on the counter rather than handing it to her.

She put her open text book down as if it were an excruciating effort then snatched the cigarettes from the rack behind her and tossed them on the counter. I was fuming.

After she *dropped* the change onto my open palm, I felt like I was giving her a zinger by saying, "I'll need matches too." Touché.

She fished a book out of a cigar box, slid it in front of me then hid behind her book once again. I bit my tongue and stormed toward the door. When I closed the door behind me, I slammed it so damn hard it bounced against its old wooden jamb three times.

Minutes later I parked the van alongside the trailer and stepped across the tiny grass patch to Julie's porch. When I went inside and knocked on the trailer door I could smell the delicious aroma of fresh seafood wafting from an open window.

"My, don't we look snazzy?" Julie teased after opening the door.

She was wearing this cute little white apron around her waist. All frilly around the edges it's red, block lettering shouted, **"OUTTA MY KITCHEN!"** She also had on snug jean shorts and a powder blue, man-tailored shirt. I know that may not sound like the most attractive outfit in the world but with the way Julie Albright filled it out, well, if you're a man you know exactly what I'm talking about here.

"How are you doing, Julie?" I said, stepping inside and handed her the bottle of Sangria.

"Why, thank you, Sonny! Want a glass? Dinner won't be ready for a few minutes yet."

"Nah ... not right now. Maybe with dinner."

"I hope you like seafood." she said, turning to the stove, flipping over some sizzling golden fillets.

"You bet I do. And this looks every bit as good as it smells."

"It's fresh permit. Buster's charter caught it today. They're staying at a motel and don't have cooking facilities so they gave the fish to Buster. He cleaned it and dropped these off this afternoon."

"How was he?" I asked in a concerned voice laced with guilt.

"He seemed preoccupied. I could tell the gears were turning in his head. He didn't stay long, just gave me the fish and said he had to go back and clean the boat."

Noticing a clean ashtray on the tiny snack bar alongside to the stove, I sat on one of the two rattan stools and lit a cigarette. I inhaled, let out a thin plume of smoke then said with finality, "I've decided what I'm going to do, Julie."

Turning from the stove abruptly, as if she'd been waiting on pins and needles to hear what I planned to do, she asked, "And, what would that be?"

"Well, there's only one thing I can do. If I want to be able to live with myself, I've got to stick with Buster all the way. When I was growing up back in Queens I never once even *considered* not helping a friend who needed it. Sure, there were always possible consequences, and a lot of times they weren't very promising, but my friends and I had an unwritten code. We helped each other out of a lot of jams on those New York streets. And it's no different now ... here with Buster. I'm sorry, but that's just the way I am."

More than a little ticked at my decision, her happy look all but gone by now, Julie said, "Code! Come on Sonny! That sounds like some kind of unwritten macho law?"

"No, Julie, it's much, much more than a code or a law. It comes from the heart. Somebody messes with your close friends or family, helping them – no matter what the consequences, is a reflex from within." Starting to tap myself on the chest with my index finger now, I added, "And I like Buster. He, his father, everybody around here are good people."

Relenting just a tad now, Julie said, "Okay, what you're saying is admirable. I'll give you that. But I still think the police should be handling this."

There was a short pause in our conversation then. Just outside the trailer a mockingbird let out a litany of squawks. It was as if the bird was giving us hell for having a disagreement. Julie and I just looked at each other. I watched what was left of her perturbed look melt away.

"What do you say," she finally said, "are you hungry? Dinner's ready."

We ate the fried fish along with conch fritters, brown rice and spinach. It was out of this world, and so was the homemade conch chowder. As I scarfed mine down, I twice told Julie how delicious everything was. Right after the second time, when I was secretly comparing her cooking with Wendy's, and thinking about Julie's hidden left hand, the telephone rang.

Quickly dabbing her lips with a napkin, Julie went

to the counter and picked the wireless up.

"Hello! Oh, hi Pa! No, no I haven't. Not since about three o'clock when he dropped off some fish here. He didn't stay long, and when he left he said he was going to clean the boat."

Julie then glanced at the starburst clock on her living room wall. "No," she said, lifting a long strand of black hair from her eye, "he didn't say a thing about it."

"Is Pa at the bar?" I blurted out.

Julie nodded her head at me in small quick bounces and furrowed her eyebrows.

"Yes. He is here, Pa."

Jumping to my feet then, I said "Tell him I'm coming right over!"

Chapter 15

Julie hung up the phone and declared, "I'm going with you."

"Come on, are you losing it. This could get nasty. I don't think you should."

"Sonny, I *want* to go," she said sternly then softened her voice some, "I'll stay out of the way. I promise."

It was obvious that no matter how much I resisted she was going.

"Damn it you're stubborn. Alright, let's go. There's no time to be arguing."

As we rushed over to Barnacle Bell's in my van, I let her in on a few more of the details I'd learned from Cap and Dalton the night before at Hugs & Jugs. She told me that Pa had said it wasn't like Buster to miss supper. He'd have at least called to let his father know if he wasn't going to make it.

When we got to the bar the old man's face grew pale and the trenches in his forehead deepened as I told him about that madman, Brock Blackburn. Buster only told Pa that we had picked up a lead in Key West, and that he was almost certain Lionel Topper was involved. All he'd said other than that was that he wanted to investigate further to be sure.

"Are you sure he didn't say anything else?" I asked Pa, wondering if Buster told him that I'd backed out of helping him.

"No, that was it."

Relieved as all hell I then thought, *That Buster's a pretty shrewd ole boy! I'll bet he knew all along that I'd be with him. I never should have suspected he would tell anybody how I wiggled my way out of the jam last night. He's got too much class for that.*

"We're going down to Stock Island, Pa. Blackburn lives there. That's got to be where he went – either there or Hugs & Jugs. Come on, Julie. If you're still going to insist on coming, let's go!"

"Hold on just a bit," Pa said, holding his palm up like a traffic cop. "Wait here for a sec."

He then snatched a brown paper bag from behind the bar and hustled to his small office in back. Julie and I glanced at each other quizzically then I looked around the bar. Sweet Home Alabama was playing on the jukebox. The redhead from the supermarket was back with her friend. This time they were rapping away with four shrimpers in white rubber boots. That's all I noticed because that quickly Pa came back out. Walking towards us, around the outside of the bar, he jerked his head at the door and said, "C'mon, outside."

Another one of those fast moving Florida thunder storms had moved in from the west, and it was beginning to come down pretty hard.

"Take this," Pa said, handing me the brown bag.

It was weighty. I looked inside and there was a handgun – a 38 caliber. Now holding the bag if it were contaminated, I felt my stomach tighten and my teeth clamp together.

"Sonny," Pa said, "forget that you even have it. It's only in case you get into a jam."

The rain started pouring down then. Heavy drops drummed on the roof of the building as I said, "Okay, Pa, you go back inside. We're going to head down there. As soon as we get back we'll let you know what we found out."

"Maybe we should drive by your house first," Julie said hopefully. "Maybe he's home now."

"Nah," Pa said, shaking his head, rain dripping from his bushy white brows, "I called one last time when I went into the office for the piece. Still no answer."

Julie and I bolted through the rain to my van. Once inside, both of us soaked to the skin, I leaned over to deposit the firearm into a slide-out storage compartment beneath the passenger seat. As soon as Julie saw me leaning toward it, she quickly, reflexively, curled the remaining fingers of her hand into her palm. Little did she know that ever since we'd gotten back on good terms I'd been making a point of not looking at that hand.

Nasty lightening – blinding cloud-to-ground strikes – snapped all around as we drove south through the now dark Keys. One time, just a hundred feet ahead on the road's shoulder, a ball of fire exploded six feet above the grass. Its light, like a small explosion, brightly illuminated the green leaves of some mangrove trees.

Both of us flinching, I said, "Oh shit! Did you see that?"

"How could I not? Look at that smoke where it hit."

The torrential rain made visibility almost non-existent. I tightened my damp grip on the wheel then leaned towards the windshield as a set of oncoming headlights approached. After they passed by us, I seriously considered pulling onto the road shoulder and waiting for the storm to pass. But I didn't. We needed to get where we were going pronto, even though it was impossible to drive faster than twenty-five miles per hour. As I plowed on into the storm and darkness, Julie and I were too deep in our own disturbing thoughts to say much. The few times we did talk it was in a rat-a-tat-tat, rapid-fire exchange of nervous words. By the time we approached the Boca Chica Channel Bridge neither of us had uttered a single word for at least ten minutes, or so it seemed. But, just as we drove onto the structure, we finally came out of the rain and Julie broke that silence.

"God," she said, turning her face toward me, "Buster better be alright. He doesn't deserve any of this crap."

"No he doesn't. I don't know if we're going to find him down here, but I just feel like we have to keep moving, looking – doing something. There was no way I was going to just sit around Wrecker's and wait."

With the rain behind us now and the roads dry we got to Hugs and Jugs in no time. Slowly we motored through several rows of parked cars and pickups, my eyes flicking back and forth at each and every one of them. After checking out the main parking area in front of the dive, I had to stop short for two men. Seemingly appearing out of nowhere, they swayed and stumbled their way through the beams of my headlights. Now they were in no hurry. Both of them dressed in grungy work uniforms they then stopped for a moment – right smack in front of my van. All lit up now, in more ways than one, they each took a slug from the same bottle of cheap rum. One said something; they laughed hysterically, patted each other's back, slipped fives, and only then finally headed for the doorway again. They didn't know we existed. Julie and I just shook our heads as I steered around to the side of the building. Buster's truck wasn't there either. Neither was Topper's Benz nor Blackburn's burgundy beater.

As soon as I turned back onto the boulevard I glanced at Julie. Still silent, her distraught face was lit a surreal pink from the giant neon dancer on the sign to her right. I was even sorrier now that I had allowed her to come along. I hated the idea of bringing her to where I had to go next.

"I knew that would be too easy," I said as we picked up speed. "Now there's no choice. As much as I hate to we've *got* to go Stock Island and look around there."

Buster had told me there were some really trashy trailer parks on Stock Island. And that he'd bet anything Blackburn was holed up in one of them. He also said a couple of those parks were so nasty that even the local police made every possible effort to avoid them at night.

A few blocks past the "Purple Conch" – that sleazy saloon Buster had pointed out to me the night before, we came up on a rundown trailer park. When we reached the far end of it, I turned right off of US 1 then made another right onto the first narrow, unlit street running through the park. I did not want to be where I was, particularly with Julie sitting alongside me. I deeply regretted caving into her. When she had insisted on coming with me at the bar, I should have put my foot down. I should have said no.

With the van's windows wide open, I slowly drove through a tight maze of small, rickety trailers. Most had lights on and windows open. Here and there, a few of the more fortunate residents had small air-conditioners jutting from their windows.

"We're looking for a '67 or '68 Chevy pickup, burgundy," I said, as I carefully steered between two tight rows of time-worn jalopies. "Do you know what they look like?"

"Not really, but I'll know what an old burgundy pickup looks like when I see one."

"Good point. I'm sorry ... I'm just a little uptight is all."

"Oh, Sonny, I'm scared sick for Buster."

"I don't like the smell of things either, but let's not let our minds run away with themselves right now. The first thing we have to do is try to ... " Right then my mouth suddenly froze and I stopped talking midsentence. I noticed something in the conical beam of my headlights. It was down at the end of the road – parked on a cross street – the side of a pickup truck. Still saying nothing, I craned my neck forward toward the windshield. My heart started thumping uncontrollably. I thought it would bust through my rib cage. I could feel my pulse pounding in my temples as well.

"What is it?" Julie blurted in a tone jolting with concern. "What in hell's the matter?"

It was a red pickup, and definitely a Ford.

Immediately I stomped down on the gas pedal and the words gushed out of me.

"UP AHEAD – IT'S BUSTER'S TRUCK!"

With hot adrenalin flooding my arms, I jockeyed through the passageway of cars faster than the most reckless of New York taxi drivers.

Buster's pickup was parked perpendicular to the road, on a grassy shoulder skirting a canal. It was desolate back there, and both doors were wide open. The rays from the van's headlights shone clear through the empty cab, penetrating the haunting mangroves behind it and settling on the pitch-black water.

I killed the lights, yanked the steering wheel hard to the left and pulled onto the grass in front of the truck.

"Hand me that gun, Julie!" I said, slamming the gearshift into park before killing the engine.

"I don't like this one bit!" she said as she bent over and carefully fished the loaded gun out of the storage compartment behind her feet.

"Not now, Julie!" I demanded in a loud, no-nonsense whisper.

Fully extending her arm, she held the heavy paper bag out as if it were a bomb that could go off at any second.

"See if there's a flashlight in there too," I whispered in a lower tone now as my eyes searched beneath the moonlit trees outside the van.

Julie quickly sifted through road maps, spare fuses, an owner's manual and whatever else I had in there before coming up with the flashlight. She turned it on, but it was a no go.

"Let me see it," I said.

With shaky hands I unscrewed the lens and rearranged the batteries – still nothing. I gave it a couple of quick raps on my open hand but that didn't get it to work either. Dropping the useless thing headfirst into a drink holder between the seats, I said, "Come on!"

We dashed through the weeds and sandspurs over to Buster's truck. I put my hand on its hood – still warm. It hadn't been parked there long.

“Oh God! Blood!” Julie yelped, as she touched a dark, wet steak on the vinyl passenger seat.

“Shhh!” I said, switching off the safety on the Smith and Wesson.

Other than the muffled sound of a television coming from one of the trailers back up the road, the only thing audible was the faint buzz of a revved up outboard somewhere out on the dark channel. An outsized full moon helped us see through the tangles of branches and mangrove roots – out to a narrow strip of shoreline along the water. The damned no-see-ums were everywhere. Continually swatting at a cloud of them in front of my perspiring face, I pushed through the mangroves to the shoreline. Julie was right behind me.

We’d only taken a few steps along the water’s edge when she tapped me firmly on the shoulder, twice. As I stopped and turned to her, she raised an index finger said in a spooked whisper, “Listen. What’s that?’”

There was an ever-so-slight rustling in the mangroves. It only lasted a second or two and then it stopped. Standing dead still with our eyes locked on each other’s, we strained to hear.

“Maybe a raccoon or something,” I said in a hushed voice.

"Shhh! I don't think so!"

Then we heard something else – a weak, barely-distinguishable wheeze.

Then it ceased.

Julie's eyes were open so wide now I could see the moon's reflection in them. Brushing her back gently with one arm, I drew the 38 and pointed it at whatever was in there. We took a couple of tentative steps back into the mangrove trees, and then we saw it! A man was lying in there, among the countless long, airborne roots that had been exposed by the receded tide. He was big man, a big *motionless* man, and he was flat on his back in the darkness.

Moving forward one more step, holding onto a thick limb with one hand for support, I aimed the shaking pistol at the body just in case. Closer now, my eyes focused better, I could see long damp tangles of hair lying over his face. The wet locks were peppered with sand, and they were *blond*.

"My good god!" I cried out as if in excruciating pain, "Noooo! It's Buster!"

Chapter 16

Buster's lips were slightly parted. Rivulets of blood crawled from the corners of his mouth down both sides of his chin. His eyes were swollen shut.

I quickly bent over and pressed my trembling fingertips firmly on his neck. No pulse – nothing! I pushed harder, feeling around for his jugular. And then, when I had just about lost hope, I did found a pulse. It was ever so weak, but it *was* there.

Julie and I each grabbed a limp ankle and dragged Buster, inches at a time, out of the maze of roots and branches. We had to stop and catch our breaths a few times, but we managed to get him alongside the van. As Julie dropped to her knees beside him, weeping as if she were at his funeral, I hurriedly searched my pockets for my keys.

"Oh God!" Julie cried out. She was panting hard, trying to catch her breath while holding Buster's heavy head and pushing his hair back from his slack face. "Hurry, Sonny!"

I rushed to the back of the van, unlocked the doors and opened them wide as they would go. I don't know how I did it, let alone Julie, but by grasping Buster under his massive arms we managed to lift his bulk high enough so that his upper body rested on the van's carpeted floor. I then vaulted inside and pulled while

Julie lifted his legs. When we finally did get him inside, Julie climbed in back next to Buster saying, "I'll stay here with him."

I tore out of there like right now. Speeding recklessly, I ran every stop sign and red light until we skidded to a stop in front of the emergency entrance of the hospital.

"I'll be right back!" I told Julie without turning around. "And open those doors!"

Not taking time to close my own door behind me, I bolted for the glass entryway.

In no time at all two men who were dressed like doctors but really weren't, wheeled Buster's lifeless body inside on an aluminum gurney. I helped push the thing as well, but I did not like feeling the chill of the metal rail in my hands. Sure, I well knew it was cold because of the hospital's super-cool air-conditioning, but it put me to mind of the gurneys they used in another very cold place.

Once we got Buster inside, an ER nurse immediately fitted him with an oxygen mask and they whisked him away. As soon as he was out of sight Julie asked a nurse if she could use a telephone.

"Do you want me to call Pa?" I asked as we stood at the end of the admission counter.

"No," she said, shaking her head vigorously as she

dialed Barnacle Bell's number.

"Hello Pa," she said, looking at me for strength. "Yes, we found him, but he's hurt pretty bad. He's ... well, he's unconscious, but we're at the hospital on Stock Island. They just wheeled him away ... Okay, we'll see you when you get here. Please, Pa, be careful driving. They're going to do everything they can. The main thing is that we got him here ... Okay, bye."

"He's coming right down," Julie said, pushing aside a strand of black hair from her face.

Seeing her so frazzled with worry tore at me inside. I wanted to put my arms around her, hold her close and come up with something assuring to say, but I didn't. I just couldn't. As great as we had been getting along again, there was still a voice in my head saying, "Hold back! Don't set her up for another letdown. You know damn well you could never overlook her ... her handicap."

The best I could do was gently take her by the elbow, nod at the rows of blue plastic chairs in the waiting area, and say, "Come on, Julie. Let's sit over there."

The place reeked of antiseptic. The PA squawked out codes and called the names of doctors. RNs and LPNs dashed back and forth, orderlies pushed metal carts along the white tiled floor. It was a busy night.

Everything moved quickly – everything except the time it took for Pa to get there. All Julie and I did was sit and worry. We didn't talk much. The few times we did exchange a few words there was always a long lull in the conversation afterwards. Deep as we both dug into our minds during those silent periods, neither of us could come up with a single optimistic thing to say. No part of this horrible mess looked good. Buster; Pa, my and Julie's future together, the future of Flagler's Key, the reoccurring vision of my naked wife on my thirty-ninth birthday – all of it was weighing heavy on me.

Finally, after about a half hour, Pa came through the entrance with Jackie and Fred.

"What do you know?" Pa asked, desperately searching Julie's eyes then mine.

"He doesn't look good. We haven't heard anything yet," was all Julie could come up with.

She looked like she was going to break out in tears any second so I explained, "We went to a trailer park here on Stock Island because Cap Forest said Blackburn lived in one. We were driving through it and found Buster's pickup at the end of a road, next to a canal. We found him way back in a bunch of thick mangroves. He was ... he was barely breathing, Pa."

The scared look on thc old seaman's face intensified. I swear I could feel the cold, dark chill over his spirit thickening. Nobody said anything for a moment. I just looked down at my feet.

"Obviously you didn't have time to look for Blackburn," Jackie said, as if he were asking me a question.

"No, but he had to have been there. Both of the truck's doors were open."

"And, the passenger seat was ... it was all bloody," Julie added.

"I think Blackburn thought Buster was finished," I chimed in. "He drove over there to dump him in the canal. But Buster must have come to, and even though he was hurting, he managed to get himself out of the water. He probably thought he'd take cover in the mangroves in case Blackburn came back."

"Sounds logical," Fred Sampson said.

"I want to talk to that nurse over there," Pa said. "Be right back."

"Be careful, she's a witch! I already had it out with her," I said.

We all watched as Pa spoke to the nurse at the counter. He looked ten years older than when Julie and I had spoken to him at the bar just a few hours earlier. For the first time since I met him he wasn't standing tall and strong. Even though he had his back to us now I could see his shoulders were hunched forward and his head was slung real low. The way he had both hands flat on the mica counter, I thought he might have needed the extra support to hold himself up.

When Pa turned around and walked back over to us he looked as though he'd been drained of all his blood.

"He's very critical," he said, and a tear fell onto the white-tiled floor. Julie put her arms around him and held him as he went on, "His skull's fractured. He's got some broken ribs too ... one of 'em punctured a lung, and he's got contusions all over his body. It, it doesn't look good. He's in a coma. Excuse me."

Gently he withdrew himself from Julie's arms. With his head still hanging low, he walked directly outside to the parking lot. Tears were streaming his worried face.

"Let's give him some space," Jackie said, "I've seen a lot of grieving relatives react to trauma when I was on the job in Brooklyn. Pa's got to let the initial shock and emotion drain itself, then he'll start to regain strength and hope. It's gotta run its course."

"He's strong, but he's also old," Julie said. Her eyes were all welled up too. "What would he do if Buster d ... if something happened to him?"

"For starters, let's just hope for the best," I said. "If, God forbid, the worst were to happen we'll deal with it then. In the meantime, Buster's still alive. And he's where he needs to be."

"You're right," Fred added. "Let's try not to put ourselves through any additional emotional burdens before they're necessary."

Julie had been glancing back and forth at those glass doors. Now, quickly dabbing her eyes with a Kleenex, she said, "Here comes Pa. Let's be strong for him."

"Sit here, Pa," I said when he rejoined us. "How about I run out and try to find some fresh coffee?"

Pa did sit down. Then the old conch looked up at me through glazed, red eyes and said, "Thanks anyway, why don't you all get back to Wreckers and get some sleep instead? I'm gonna stay here the night."

None of us challenged his wishes. We looked at each other, nodding in agreement, and then Julie said, "O.k., Pa. Sure. But you call me later if you change your mind, I'll come right back down and get you. Otherwise, I'll be back in the morning."

Pa agreed, and we all shuffled outside into the lighted parking lot. With our voices echoing in the still night air, we stood by Jackie's van as he boarded the wheelchair lift. When the platform began to elevate him he said, “You need to go to the police, Sonny. You know more about the bastard who’s responsible for this than any of us.”

“I know ... I’ve got to do *something*.”

Julie didn’t like the way I said that. After searching my eyes for a short moment, she slowly pronounced and spaced each word when she said, “What-do-you-mean-by-that?”

“Nothing!” I snapped. Then I said with finality, “I just want to get back to my trailer and try to get some rest. I’ve got to get up early for work tomorrow.” I blamed myself for what had happened to Buster. My only hope for a semblance of self-redemption was to somehow fix this mess.

“Don’t get any crazy ideas,” Julie said, coming off a little angry now.

“Good night, guys,” I said, putting an end to the discussion. Then I put my palm on Julie’s lower back and led her to my van.

“Good night Jackie, Fred,” Julie said, looking back at them and then at the hospital one last time.

As we drove back to Wrecker’s beneath a wide, black dome splattered with stars, we didn’t have a whole lot to say to each other. And that was fine with me. With all the toxic thoughts I had circulating in my head, I sure as hell didn't need Julie laying more pressure on me. But it was inevitable. I knew she'd want answers. Right after we passed through Cudjoe Key and were crossing the dark bridge over Kemp Channel, she turned to me and asked, "What's going on in there, Sonny? Please tell me what you think you're going to do about this."

"Nothing," I said, then, just as quickly in attempt to undo my lie I added, "I mean I don't want to talk about it right now. It's been a long night and I just want to get some sleep."

Not long later I pulled the van in between our two trailers. The headlights illuminated the woods in back startling an armadillo. It bolted as quickly as armadillos can into the palmettos, and I shut off the engine and had to tap the gas pedal twice again. I started to climb out but then stopped. Julie was just sitting there, looking at me.

"What?" I asked, quizzically.

She didn't say anything for a moment. Even with my door open it was dead quiet. She just looked across the dark van at me then finally she raised her hand, put it on my shoulder and massaged it. "Don't go looking for this psycho, Sonny! Please, I'm groveling here, just turn it over to the sheriff's department."

"Julie, I don't know which end is up right now,

okay? I've got thoughts and ideas buzzing in and out of my head so fast that I can't make sense out of any of them. My mind's been like that a lot lately. Nothing stays in there long enough to figure any of it out."

"Okay, I understand. Get some sleep, but please ... consider turning it over to the police."

I could tell she wanted to put her arms around me and kiss me. That much I can read from the look in a woman's eyes. But she didn't. She just turned and then got out of the van.

"Do me a favor, "I said to her back, "Call me at the shop tomorrow and let me know how Buster's doing."

She stopped for a second, turned around, said, "Sure. Good night," then turned back around and stepped into her porch.

Chapter 17

The next morning I got two personal phone calls while working at the tackle shop. The first was ten minutes after I'd opened up. It was Cap Forest. I hadn't seen or heard from him since the night at Mugs and Jugs, so I told him how Julie and I found Buster on Stock Island and what ensued afterwards. After filling him in on everything, he said he wanted to tell me a little more about Brock Blackburn. He said there hadn't been enough time at the strip joint and he hadn't been in any condition to think straight that night anyway. After that, he told me that he had known an inmate at Raiford who seemed to know quite a bit about Brock Blackburn. Then Cap told me everything he knew.

He said the killer's long, coarse black hair somehow seemed artificial and that it framed his hard face like a cheap wig. It was a face that hid some horrible stories in its teardrops. There was a horseshoe shaped scar on his right cheek, his nose was crooked at the bridge, and there were always deep, angry creases between his eyebrows. Below those thick black brows were two vacant, forbidding eyes – dead eyes – eyes that conveyed his unnerving ruthlessness.

Cap also went on to tell me that when Blackburn was a kid, his old man often came home drunk to their dilapidated house and liked to give the oldest of his six sons a good pounding. The youngest two boys, none of which bore any resemblance to each other, used to walk unsupervised around the old house either bare-assed naked or in filthy underpants. It seemed there was never any money left for clothes because of the family patriarch's drinking habit and the payments he made on his new Mercury. As for Blackburn's mother and older sister, they were no help either. Just like the old man, they were hardly ever home. Most nights they'd be out *together*, soliciting their bodies. Cap said that although he didn't know if it were true, there had been a rumor circulating in prison that many nights the mother and daughter would service the same John – together. It seemed they were a tag-team of sorts.

Nevertheless young Brock's didn't last forever. They came to an abrupt end on an unusually cold South Florida Christmas Eve. While sitting alone in the darkness of the front room, fifteen-year-old Brock had gotten up the nerve to drink almost two full six-packs of his old man's Busch beer. Groggy, but with a new-found confidence, he waited for his father to come home. On the floor alongside him there was a cinderblock he'd stolen that afternoon from a construction site out on State Road 84.

*****

It was just shy of midnight when the senior

Blackburn pulled his shiny Merc into the driveway. Brock, who had almost fallen asleep by then, snapped to attention when he heard the crunch of gravel beneath wheels and saw slashes of white light cutting through a metal jalousie window he'd left open a crack. Coolly, slowly, he picked up the cement block, and crept to the side of the doorway.

After his father entered the house and closed the door the teenager came at him in the darkness, slamming the heavy block into the back of his neck. Blackburn had told that other inmate in Raiford that when he heard his old man's neck crack and watched the bastard drop to the floor he felt a strange sense of exhilaration that he'd never felt before. He'd also added that it felt just as good when he then stomped on his father's chest and felt his ribs splinter under the force of his foot.

Brock Blackburn left home that night, never to return. Two days later, the cops found him sleeping under the bleachers at an elementary school baseball field near downtown Fort Lauderdale. He was sent away to reform school, where he had the very first teardrop tattooed beneath his eye.

After Cap told me all that, I asked him if he knew where Lionel Topper lived. He said it just so happened he did. Less than a year earlier Topper had chartered his boat and paid him with a check. He'd looked at the address on the check and knew it was in a gated community in Key West, a place called

"Dolphin Estates".

Just minutes after thanking him and hanging up the phone I got that second call. I was damn glad for the distraction too. My mind was in a panic. There is no easy way of describing how petrified I was. All I can tell you is that when you know that you just might end up dealing with a cold, heartless lunatic like Blackburn, who enjoys hearing necks snap the way he does, it doesn't leave a whole hell of a lot of room in your mind for happy thoughts.

"Hello," I said into the phone, as I sat on the backless stool behind the counter, "Big Time Bait & Tackle."

"Good morning, Sonny."

It was Julie. And her tone was about as upbeat as my thoughts were. My palms suddenly moistened and knees started doing that bouncing thing again.

"Are you at the hospital?"

"Yes, I'm here with Pa. Sonny, he looks so old and helpless. He's been here all night. His white hair is all disheveled, and you can see most of his eyelids. He can barely keep them open. His clothes are rumpled up and there's a coffee stain from last night right on the front of his tee shirt. He just doesn't ...."

"Julie," I interrupted, "how's Buster?"

“It’s not encouraging. His blood pressure is still way too low, and as you know, he’s got a concussion, broken ribs and that punctured lung. He’s on a life support machine ... still in a coma.”

“What’s the doctor say? Are you telling me he’s not going to come out of this?”

“He’s got an excellent doctor. His name’s Ryerson, best neurologist in the Keys. He said the longer he ... he’s in a coma, the greater the chance he could have brain damage. Sonny, I’m sorry, I’m trying to be strong for Pa, but I’m going to lose it here. I’m going to cry. I can’t help myself.”

“Don’t be silly, Julie. It’s okay. Look, do you want me to close the shop and come down there?”

“No,” she answered with a sniffle now, “it’s alright. There’s nothing you can really do here. It’s just that Buster looks so helpless lying in that bed – all hooked up to so many wires and tubes. He looks terrible, Sonny. I’m scared.”

I’d been stroking my chin as Julie had been speaking. Now that she was finished I propped myself up on the stool and, as if a switch had been thrown, the ominous fear I’d been enveloped in suddenly turned into anger. I was pissed – totally fed up with the whole thing.

“I’ll tell you what, Julie,” I snapped into the

phone, "right now I'm just inches from getting in my van, going the fuck down there, and blowing away both those bastards – Blackburn *and* Topper!"

"Sonny," she pleaded desperately, "don't be ... "

"Don't worry!" I interrupted. "As much as I want to, I'm not going to do anything right this minute. I'm going to sit tight. But I'll tell you this, and I promise you, if Buster doesn't come out of this okay, by God I *will* handle it."

"Look, let's not get into that now. Why don't we take one thing at a time? I still think you and Pa ought to be turning this over to the Sheriff's Department, but I'm glad you at least decided not to do anything crazy right now. Sonny ... " she paused then on the other end, as if searching for the words that would follow and lining them up in their proper order, "I think you well know by now that I, I ... well, hell, I think you know that I really care about you. I think you care about me as well. A woman can read those kinds of things. But I also know there's something standing in your way. I know what it is, Sonny. I wish I could do something to change that, but I can't. Okay ... there, I said it. I've been wanting to get that off my chest for a while now. But please, don't say anything right now. I don't want to talk about it. I just wanted you to know that I know."

I was stunned. Feeling as if I'd just been hit by a mortar round, I leaned back on that stool. If there hadn't been wooden shelving behind me, I would have gone over backwards. I struggled for the right words to say but had no idea what the hell they would be. Trying to sound as nonchalant as I possibly could, the best I could do was stutter, "Y-Y-Yeah, well ah ... your right. I think the best thing to do about Buster is sit back and see what transpires. Look Julie," I then lied, "I've got to get off the phone now. There's a customer coming in. I'll talk to you later, alright?"

"Sure. Would you like to stop over for coffee or a beer when you get home? I mean if you don't have any plans or anything."

"How about I stop over for coffee in the morning? I'm dog-tired after last night."

"Sure, that would be great," she said, but her words were drenched with disappointment.

Sitting there with the phone to my ear, I thought how the best people always make the poorest liars. And as that ran through my head, I said, "If you hear anything about Buster – anything at all, good or bad, please let me know. Otherwise I'll see you in the AM."

"Of course I will. Goodbye."

Totally drained by nine o'clock that night, I sacked out early. I needed to be well-rested for the next day – for whatever might be waiting for me. As I lay there beneath a thin sheet in the darkness, I heard the single high-pitched “KWAWK” of a yellow-crowned night heron somewhere out in the mangroves. Then, right after that, came the “hoot, hoot, hoot, hoot” of an owl somewhere in the jungle back behind the trailer.

After the owl’s second series of hoots my eyelids met, and I again thought about what Julie had said on the phone. It hurt to think how she bared her soul to me – come right out and told me how much she really cared, and I wasn’t able do the same. She’d said there was something holding me back and, of course, she was a hundred percent right. But no matter how hard I tried, and I had been trying for quite some time, I just couldn’t get past that hand thing. Sure, she had a heart big as a setting sun in the tropics, and a face that was even more beautiful. But I was sure I knew myself. And for the first time I was *dead* sure that I couldn’t possibly spend the rest of my life with Julie Albright. That realization certainly didn’t bring me any peace though. For the longest time I just lay there – self-hate stabbing at me until, finally, I drifted off to sleep. But even then there was no serenity.

As I had so many times since our ugly breakup, I dreamed of Wendy and how things were when we first started dating. How carefree life was and how I anticipated being with her every minute that I wasn’t. I’d think of her while driving my old Plymouth, while at school and when at home with my parents. I lived for that girl, and she lived for me. Our relationship added a whole new dimension to my life. I was alive in every sense of the word; no longer just a solitary person living an incomplete existence. My life had become larger than that. I was bubbling over with youthful dreams and had somebody to share them with. Lovely as this dream sounds it was a cruel dream as well. Because I always woke up from it feeling empty inside – alone, missing that other part of myself that had betrayed me. Sure, those loving feelings I had for Wendy were gone by now, but the happy memories of *us* would never be. And it was those treasured remembrances that caused my lasting pain.

I had been into the dream for quite a while when something jarred me awake. There were sounds outside the trailer – noises really, strange unnatural noises off in the distance that I'd never heard on the Key. Motionless, still not totally conscious, I lay there in the blackness straining to hear. Then something clicked in my mind. It was engines that were tainting the nighttime quiet – big powerful ones, and they weren't very far away.

As if an air raid siren had gone off, I sprung out of that bed; hot footed it through the trailer to the front room, backhanded both curtains open at once, and peered out beyond the channel.

I didn't have to look long or far. Like a swarm of white fireflies, lights flickered on and off as they made their way through the brush on Flagler's Key. It was them! They had come! Lionel Topper's midnight dozers were clearing their way through the bushes and trees. Bright beams of light crisscrossed in the darkness as the destructive machines began to level the natural, wild beauty of the island. Surely, all the nearby animals – the key deer, coons, birds, and armadillos were fleeing the monstrous steel predators, some possibly abandoning their young.

That son of a bitch, Topper! He didn't even wait! He's leveling the key before they even had change of zoning hearing.

I dashed back to the bedroom and with shaky hands pulled on a shirt and shimmied into the first pair of shorts I could get my hands on. After hastily tying my sneakers, I grabbed my wallet and keys from the night stand and bolted out the door. There were lights on in most of the nearby trailers, including Julie's. As I rushed to the door of my van, I hadn't seen her standing out in front of her place in a terrycloth robe.

"Sonny, wait! Where are you going? Come ...."

"I can't talk, Julie! Got to get to Pa's! There's no time to waste!" I shouted as I climbed into the bucket seat.

I then cranked up the van, peeled out of there, and sped over the bumpy road to Pa's house. A couple of minutes later I skidded to a stop in front of his yard.

As I raced up the path to the house that the owl hooted again when the entire nighttime sky suddenly lit up like daylight. I dashed around the side, passed the cistern then saw Pa in the brilliant white light. Standing out on the dock in only his boxer shorts, pointing a flare gun toward Flagler's Key, he discharged another one. "YOU RAPIST SONS OF BITCHES!" he hollered in a strained, hoarse voice as the white flare arched way out over the water like a comet.

He then started to reload the gun but looked up when he heard my heavy footsteps running toward him on the wooden planking.

"They're doing it Pa!" I said a moment later, as I slammed into the dock's wooden railing alongside him. "The bastards are ...."

I didn't finish that sentence. I stopped talking right there when I turned to look at Pa. His shoulders were sagging as far as they'd go, and so was his heart. The old man was looking me in the eyes as if screaming for help. His tears had already made their way all the way to his jawbone, on both sides of his face. One fell to the wood below. This man who had stood strong against injustice for eighty years was now broken. It freaking tore at my heart to see him like this. To say I saw red would be an understatement – I saw crimson, a dark, angry shade of it that I'd only seen one other time in my life.

"Pa!" I told him, grabbing onto his perspiring shoulders and shaking them, "Go call the sheriff – right now! I'm going over there. You go ahead and call them. You have to!" Then I tore back to the van.

I barreled down the bumpy road even faster than I had come up it. Speeding through the dark tropical jungle; following my high beams through that impossible tangle of palmettos, tall trees, and long, dangling vines, I kept bouncing out of my seat – twice so high that I grazed my head on van's roof.

After finally reaching Pa's store, I slowed to a stop alongside the deserted highway, jerked my head both ways, stomped down on the gas pedal then yanked the van into hard a left turn. But I didn't go far. Mere seconds later, just as I sped over the bridge's summit, a pair of blinding high beams came barreling in my direction. The car blew right by me, but not so fast that I couldn't make out the plate on its front bumper. In what felt like a nanosecond, I read it through squinted eyes. It screamed out, "WATERFRONT." Lionel Topper was hauling ass from the scene.

"The flares spooked him!" I blurted out in a nervous yet psyched-up, adrenaline-fueled tone.

When I reached the other side of the bridge, the entire fleet of yellow, destructive vehicles was frantically hightailing it out of the woods. Some of the Caterpillars and Komatsus were already being loaded onto trailers and flatbed trucks. The deafening noise and cone-shaped beams of light illuminating the rising clouds of dust only added to the confusion. Truck drivers and dozer operators were rushing in every conceivable direction. I figured Topper must have hired every excavation crew from Key West to Homestead so that he could finish his clandestine mission in a single night.

With all the activity that was going on, I don't know how many vehicles I had to drive past before coming to a clear section of the road shoulder. When I did, I swung the van so hard into a U-turn it listed to one side as it skidded onto the marl shoulder on the opposite side of the road. After showering one of the dozers with pebbles and shell fragments, I spun back onto the two-lane. I must have looked like a Hollywood stunt driver. My front tires met the asphalt road again, they squealed like two spinning banshees, the van lurched forward, and the stink of burnt rubber was everywhere. With my window wide open, I could even smell it in the van. But there was no time to think about all that. Feeling the muscles tightening and undulating in both my jaws, I accelerated as fast as I could push the van – 60, 70, 80, 90, 100 miles an hour I got it up to. The broken highway lines blurred solid as the headlights illuminated them and the van swallowed them up. There was still no sign of Topper up ahead, but I wasn't slowing down. I was hell-bent on catching him. And my infuriation only intensified with each passing mile marker.

After rounding a gradual curve, my eyelids clicked as I strained to see down the road. Taking one hand off the wheel for just a moment, I quickly massaged my pulsating temples. Then there was another curve. When I came out of that one my view was no longer obstructed by the seemingly endless row of mangrove trees alongside the dark road. That's when I spotted the Benz's red tail lights up ahead. Pushing the needle to a hundred-and-ten for the next couple of miles, I was beginning to close the gap. But then it dawned on me – what the hell was I going to do if I caught up to him out there in the boondocks? Run the bastard off the road and into the shallows of Similar Sound? I slowed down, just barely keeping his lights in my sight, and pondered my next move.

I didn't think I was ready to kill. Yet that *was* an option. In my past life I would never have entertained such a thought. But now things were different. Now the possibility didn't seem all that remote. And it scared me as I motored down that highway. *How*, I wondered *had my regard for human life diminished so much?* Was it solely because Topper had delivered Buster to death's door? Or was part of the reason that since losing Wendy I had less regard for my *own* life?

That thought and several others I didn't like stayed with me until I reached Stock Island. Once there, I backed as far off from Topper as I dared. I sure didn't want to let him out of my line of vision, but I didn't want to spook him either. I could have easily caught up to him at that point but had already decided to tail Topper to wherever the hell he was heading instead. I'd also decided on something else. I may not have known exactly what I was going to do when I confronted him, but I did know that I was going to let my pent-up hate and anger for the cretin determine that. As poor a decision as that might turn out to be, I just didn't care anymore. I was sticking to it.

At this late hour there was next to no traffic on the island. All the businesses were closed except for The Purple Conch, and that looked like it was just about ready to close. When I flicked my head to the side while passing it, I saw only three cars parked next to the building and two lost souls straddled to the bar on the inside.

It wasn't long before we approached the Holiday Inn in Key West. There was a traffic light there and the road split. At that point I edged a little closer to the black Mercedes. The light was green, but I wasn't about to watch Topper cruise right through it then get stuck for it myself. A moment later he did make it through. He veered to the left of the split in the road and closer than ever behind him I goosed the accelerator and just made it through as the light turned yellow. A few blocks later he turned by a subtly lit sign. It said, "Dolphin Estates". He was going home.

I didn't turn. I drove right by, made a U-turn at the next side street then slowly motored back toward the sign. By the time I turned into the upscale community,

Topper was out of sight. I picked up speed hoping to spot him before he garaged his car. If I didn't, there was no way I'd be able to find his house. There must have been fifty of them in there, all set back off the circular road.

With my eyes clicking back and forth stealthily, I looked down each driveway. I wanted to corner the bastard right then. There wasn't going to be any coming back, looking for him another time. I had decided that if I didn't lose it totally when we came eye to eye. I was at least going tell him that Buster was still alive. That he had fingered Blackburn, and when the chips were all down, Blackburn would finger him. If that was the way it went, I was going to then drive straight to the police station and tell them the entire story. That was the plan that was running through my mind when I suddenly saw something at the far end of the circular road.

It was the rear end of Topper's car. He had pulled into his driveway but stopped in it instead of garaging the car. The lights were out but with the aid of the fancy street lanterns above, I could see his silhouette inside. Sitting motionless in the driver's seat, his head was turned my way. He had been waiting and watching.

Now I was confused. Did he have a gun? Why in the hell would he stop within plain view when he had more than enough time to at least pull up to his garage?

Maybe he's taunting me! Maybe this clown is more dangerous than I thought. I'd better be damned careful here.

Ever so slowly now, I idled the van up to the curb just beyond the driveway, came to a stop then eased it into park. That's when all hell broke loose!

Suddenly two headlights came around the curve in front of me so fast they looked like a pair of impossibly bright shooting stars. Whoever was driving was in a big hurry, and in the blink of an eye he screeched to a halt, right smack in front of me. I couldn't see anything – nothing but those two blinding high beams lighting up my face and the inside of the van. We were grill to grill, bumper to bumper. A second later the lights went out.

At first I had thought it was the police, but now I could see in the beams of my own headlights that this was no lawman. Looking above the high hood, through the windshield of what I now realized was a pickup truck I saw the driver's face. Wow, I was sorry I did. It was the face of a demon – the most evil looking human being to ever taint my vision. Without question I knew it was that maniacal killer, Brock Blackburn.

Chapter 18

God dammit! I thought, slamming the heels of my hands on the steering wheel. *Topper called him on his cell! What am I going to do now?*

From behind the steering wheel of his Chevy, Blackburn's thin lips then widened into a cockeyed, diabolical smile. In the glow of my lights, with his badly neglected teeth and deranged face all too visible, he lit up like some kind of evil, surreal jack-o-lantern.

I'd seen enough! I yanked the gear shift into reverse and jerked my head around to back out of there – pronto.

But it was a no go. I hadn't seen him, but Topper had already backed out onto the street and stopped inches from my rear bumper. I was sandwiched!

Oh shit! This is it! All but resigned to my demise I slid the gearshift into park.

Blackburn took his sweet time getting out of the truck. Then, as if he was enjoying the moment to no end and wanted to drag it out as long as possible, he slowly swaggered to the front of the truck, stepped onto his front bumper and mine, and started walking across them – staring through my windshield at me with that god-awful smile as he did. That's when I noticed the pistol in his hand.

There was no time now to fish beneath the passenger seat for Pa's .38. Short as the van's hood was, if I was to duck down and reach for it Blackburn could have easily leaped off the bumpers, taken two short steps then filled me with lead before I'd ever gotten the thing out of the paper bag. All I could do was sit there. It was as if I were at the end of a dark alley, back to a wall, helplessly watching my executioner walk toward me. There was no way out. I just watched him with his long black hair all swept back, looking like a crazed rabid lion moving in for the kill. Cap Forest had said he was big, but that was an understatement. This guy was huge. Shirtless beneath an open leather vest, he looked like an insane modern-day Hercules. Never, in any gym, had I seen a man with so many networks of blue veins popping out of his muscular body.

In no time at all he was standing right beside my door. I froze. All I could do was look through the open window at that scarred up face and the teardrops beneath his left eye. But I didn't look very long. He jammed the barrel of his gun into my left temple, and I mean *jammed* it. He rammed it so hard against my skull that I saw a flash of white and thought the gun had gone off. But it hadn't.

"Okay mother fucker," he demanded in a thick southern drawl, "shut this piece a shit off now! And kill them lights."

As I climbed out of the van Topper strode up to it. Keeping my head motionless with that steel barrel still tight against it, I swept my eyes to the side and looked at him. He was already looking at me, with an arrogant prep school smirk smeared across his face. There was no time to do a lot of thinking, but out there in the amber glow of an overhead street light I couldn't decide who looked more sinister; Topper with his handsome delicate features or the towering, hulking subhuman in the vest.

As he continued to study me, Topper reached beneath his sport jacket and pulled out his own pistol. With two of them pointing at my head now he told Blackburn, "Pull the cars into the driveway – all the way to the back. I'll take our guest inside."

"Awright," Blackburn came back, "but don't go whackin' him yet. *I* want his sorry ass. I wanna do him, just like I did his asshole buddy, Bell."

Then the lunatic widened that busted up smile of his, pulled the gun away from my head and pointed it his facial tattoos. Pushing his crooked nose so close to my face that I could smell the stench of sardines or some kind of rank fish on his breath he said, "I think I'm gonna' cry again – any minute now."

"Go ahead! Let's move it!" Topper said then, shoving me toward a walkway leading to the front doors of his castle.

Dense, exotic flora snugged both sides of the stone path. Tall and professionally manicured, the dark bushes shrouded the pathway from the streetlights. It was awfully dark in there. Scoping things out as I walked, I seriously considered making a run for it. But Topper caught onto me. Noticing my inquisitiveness from behind, he well knew I wasn't just admiring the landscaping. In a low calculating voice he said from behind, "Continue walking. Don't even think about trying something."

Nevertheless, as I proceeded forward I weighed my odds of escaping outside versus inside the house. Then I heard the first vehicle idling up the driveway. It was a diesel engine. It had to be the Mercedes since it had already been nosed into the driveway. I knew then that I'd have about two minutes alone with Topper before the gorilla came busting in. I decided to take my chances inside, rather than running.

At the end of the path there was a wide set of half-moon marble steps leading up to the entranceway. Sliding a perspiring palm along one of the wrought iron handrails, I trudged to the top step.

"Move," Topper said, wagging his piece from side to side at me while reaching in his pocket for his keys. He unlocked one of the two tallest French doors I'd ever seen then shoved it open.

"After you, my friend," he said in a faux gracious tone as he extended his open hand, palm up, toward the doorway.

With my heart racing and my body perspiring profusely while contemplating my next move, I stepped into the dark, cavernous reception area.

"There's a dimmer knob on the wall – just to the left of the other door. Turn it all the way on," he ordered.

As I walked with my arms extended and palms up in the darkness, I could hear his footsteps closing in on me. With neither of us able to see worth a damn, he wanted to get up close and personal just in case he needed to fire his gun. This was it! Do or die! I needed to make my move before I got to that light switch.

With my racing heart by now in my mouth, I brought my right fist to my chest, spun around fast as I could, leaned way back, and rammed my elbow as hard as I could. It was a perfect shot. Since Topper was about my height, my elbow landed right into the side of millionaire's face. Crack! I felt the impact yet kept the momentum going. I wanted to take his freaking head off. Then a shot rang out!

I wasn't sure if I was hit or not, but when I next heard Topper's gun thud on the carpeted floor and then he went down, I knew he had taken one of his own bullets. As he lay there moaning, I dropped like a stone too. Down on my knees, leaning forward with my hands sliding – searching frantically all over the carpet like a desperate blind man, I scavenged for that gun. I couldn't find the damn thing, but the second time one my hands hit Topper's limp body he let out a wheeze. It didn't sound good, not for him anyway. Then that wheeze turned into something else, a low, raspy, god-awful rattle. I knew that for the first time in my life I was hearing what's known as "the death rattle." Topper's lights were out for good, and I couldn't have cared any less. I was damn glad he was dead.

Still without the gun, I then heard Blackburn's heavy boots stomping up the marble steps. He was taking two at a time. Forget about racing, my heart was on the verge of splitting its rib cage wide open. Lurching up and toward the door in the same motion, I tried to jump over Topper's body but didn't quite make it. I *stumbled* over him. Fighting for my balance like a first time ice skater, I took two or three quick, clumsy half steps before managing to right myself. By that time I was standing right in front of the one French door that hadn't been opened. On the other side of it, silhouetted by the dim light of the street lamp, I could now see Brock Blackburn coming.

Quickly, I scooted behind the open door and waited. About two seconds passed – the longest two of my life, then Blackburn raised a boot inside the threshold. I drew in a deep breath, tensed my entire body, waited one more fraction of a second and then did it. Leaning into the edge of that door I slammed it with every ounce of strength I had.

It was perfect! There was a loud crash the whole neighborhood would have heard had they not been sleeping. Maybe I woke them, I didn't know, all I did know was that the door nailed Blackburn head-on. But something was wrong. Instead of tumbling back like I'd hoped he would the crazed monster kept coming. He crashed through the door's glass panels as if they were made of Hollywood candy glass. He sounded like a car ramming into the plate glass windows of a Seven Eleven. With shards of glass raining into the dark house, all I could do was scrunch my eyelids closed, turn my face away, and lean harder and harder against that door.

Finally, with so much glass slicing into his face and body, Blackburn roared like a tortured beast and stumbled back a few steps. Watching through a broken pane I saw him fall off the patio backwards. His muscled back made a sickening thud as he landed on the stone steps below. Like the roar of a mortally wounded elephant in excruciating pain, his bellow was so loud that the neighbors were now surely up and running for their robes. But Blackburn wasn't mortally wounded. Two grunts later a shot rang out.

I saw the yellow flash. Wood splintered the door frame mere inches above my head. Then there was another shot, and he hollered, "You fuckin' hump, I'm coming for ya! And before I waste ya I'm gonna cut out your friggin' eyes!"

Rising to his feet now – a lot faster than I thought humanly possible, there was no time to look for Topper's gun. In no time at all Blackburn was up those steps again and heading for me. I turned and darted toward the rear of the spacious greeting room. Back by the far wall there was something that felt like a huge metal vase or urn. Quietly as I could, I pulled it out a bit and hid behind it.

BANG! BANG! BANG! Three more shots rang out in rapid succession! Still not feeling anything but raw fear, more of it than ever, I realized what Blackburn had shot at. In the darkness I heard his voice say, "Tough break *partner*! I didn't know it was you down there."

I had to act fast. I came out from behind that metal thing, felt along the wall, and almost immediately found a door. It opened and I stepped inside. Blackburn was still fumbling around in the dark too. I could hear his feet shuffling and something sliding along the walls – surely his blood-soaked hands feeling for a light switch. Then he found it and turned the rheostat all the way on.

Peeking out from the side of the doorway, I saw that a huge glass chandelier had illuminated the whole sickening scene. Squinting now, as if I'd walked out of a movie theater into bright daylight, I saw Topper lying on the floor. His body full of blood. Then, at that very moment, with the stink of burnt gunpowder still permeating my nostrils, I heard something. It was the shrill of sirens! And they weren't very far off in the distance. Monroe County Sheriff's units were speeding toward the house. The cavalry was on its way, but I still had to somehow keep myself alive. I knew it wasn't going to be easy.

"I'll get ya before they get here you bastard!" Blackburn hollered, as he plucked a sliver of sharp glass from his chin. Then he stormed toward the study door.

I slammed it closed and went to lock it, but that wasn't going to happen. There was no lock, only a keyhole. With the sound of Blackburn's Frankenstein-like steps quickly approaching the door, I scurried fast as I could across the study to a large mahogany desk I'd seen when the door had been open. I jerked the upholstered chair out hard enough so that it rolled back to the wall and I ducked beneath the desk. Then the door flew open and slammed into another wall.

Blackburn stood in the doorway for just a second; his eyes readjusting to the semi-darkness again. There wasn't much I could do, but I had to do something. I sprung up, grabbed a brass bookend I'd seen from the top of the desk, and flung it at the zombie with all I had. I missed. Blackburn turned to where it hit the wall, looked back at me and said, "I've been waiting to get you alone, *Dad.* Merry Christmas!" Then he raised his gun.

I dropped to the floor behind the desk again and rolled franticly from side to side as two more shots rang out. Then there was a click! Then click, click, click! He was out of rounds, and I was up like a cat.

Grabbing the second bookend, I raced around the desk, charged Blackburn, and slammed the thing into his butchered face. There was a distinct "crack" as the cartilage in his nose split.

"THAT ONE'S FOR BUSTER BELL!" I hollered loud as I could.

Dazed but still strong as two men, Blackburn pounced on me like an alpha lion. We went down together, but *I* was on the bottom. Crashing back-first onto the floor with all his bulk landing smack on top of me the back of my head bounced up and our foreheads collided. Instantly, I felt dazed, as if I'd fallen face first onto a concrete sidewalk. But I couldn't give up. Still face to bloody face with the raging cretin, he then took ahold of me. He bear hugged me so hard that my back was forced into an unnatural bend. The farther my spine bent into an inverted C the harder it became to breath. Fighting back the dizziness and pain, I struggled to hold onto my consciousness.

I tried to stretch my arms around the madman, but he had my shoulders restrained in his death-grip. I was being crushed by a two-hundred-and-fifty-pound vice that kept tightening and tightening. My punches were futile, like little half swings. But then, with Blackburn's snarling face so close to mine, I *just* managed to palm the sides of his grotesque face. I then extended my thumbs out as far as possible and plunged them into the killer's eyes. I pushed with all the fading strength I could muster. Deeper and deeper and deeper I forced the spongy spheres down into their sockets. "AHHHHHHHH!" he finally roared, releasing his grip on me and jerking his head back to save his eyes. But he wasn't finished.

"YOU SON OF A BITCH," he howled, "I'M GONNA FINISH YA NOW!"

He leaned forward again, shoving my arms back to the floor, and planted two knees the size of dock pilings on my elbows. That was it. I was helpless. I had no chance.

In the light from the doorway behind Blackburn, I saw him pull something from his hip. I couldn't make out what it was at first, but when he raised it in his right hand, I saw it all too clearly. With that background light flashing from its blade my executioner yelled in a horrifying hoarse voice, "I'M TAKING YOUR ... "

But that was as far as he got. At that very second an overhead light came on and Deputy Hansen G. Langford commanded, "STOP! PUT THE KNIFE DOWN! DO IT NOW!"

Blackburn spun his head around, looked over his shoulder, and shouted, "FUUUUCK YOUUUUUU!" Quickly turning back toward my terrorized face, he then drove the steel blade downward.

Three deafening shots went off in rapid succession. With my ears ringing like panicky alarms, Deputy Langford's first and third bullets struck home. The back of Blackburn's head blew wide open, splattering bloody brain tissue and skull fragments everywhere. The torso of his massive body slammed forward, coming down face first – what was left of it, right at me. Still pinned down by Blackburn's weight, I jerked my head to the side and braced myself. Then it was over.

I had to stay at Topper's house for quite some time, explaining everything to Langford and the homicide detectives. After that, in the pale rosy light of a Key West dawn, Langford put me in his squad car. They wanted to ask still more questions and have me sign some papers at the station. Sitting in the back seat as we pulled away, I turned to look at the yellow-taped crime scene one last time. All I could do was shake my head.

A few hours later, just before 9:00 AM, I was released. As I stepped out of the interrogation room and into the lobby, I pushed the hair back from my dog-tired eyes and slowly walked toward the office where I'd been told I could arrange for a ride back to my van. The place was super busy. Male and female deputies were quick-stepping in all different directions. Accusers, and the accused, were coming and going as well. It seemed as if I had to dodge every one of them as I made my way across the wide room. But then, when I was about halfway to where I was going, I saw her. It was Julie. She was sitting alone on a long wooden bench by the entrance.

Exhausted, but still alive and not defeated, I limped across the worn linoleum floor toward her. She stood up, and as I got closer I could not only see the tears welling up in her eyes, but I could feel them as well.

When I came up to her, she flung her arms around me saying, "Don't you *ever* do this to me again!"

I didn't say anything. I just pulled her close. We clung to each other in that crowded stationhouse for a long, long moment. Then, with her still in my arms, Julie leaned back and looked at me. Those welled-up tears were streaming down her face by now, but she smiled when she said, "Buster's going to make it, Sonny. The doctor called Pa a couple of hours ago and told him that he had regained consciousness. He's going to be fine."

Chills ran down both my arms as Julie leaned back up against me. Holding me even tighter this time, she laid a teary cheek against mine and said, "I dropped Pa off at the hospital then came right over here. I was worried sick about you. I didn't sleep all night and couldn't stand it any longer. When I got here, they told me what happened at Topper's house, and that, thank God, you were alright."

Gently, I lifted my cheek from hers. I looked at her, and suddenly everything seemed so clear. The deeper I looked into those caring brown eyes, the more answers I saw. I knew right then and there that it was time.

Slowly, I reached down and took her by the hand – her left hand. She looked at where they were joined and then back up at me. At long last I was content. I leaned toward her, kissed her damp cheek, smiled and said, "Come on Julie ... let's go home."

Made in the USA
Middletown, DE
27 December 2014